Dear Reader,

A couple of years ago I visited China and was overwhelmed by its beauty, its magnificence and above all its mystery. In Beijing I saw the Forbidden City, where the Emperors lived and where their concubines had their apartments. Later I visited the Terracotta Warriors. I'd heard so much about them, but nothing could have prepared me for their breathtaking, lifelike reality.

After that came a cruise along the Yangtze River, marveling at the high banks that rise on each side, giving the feeling of being enclosed in a separate world. It could be a perfect place for lovers, as my hero and heroine Lang and Olivia discovered. But at last the outside world intruded, facing them with decisions that threatened to tear them apart.

When they finally found their destiny it was because they were true to themselves and also because they had answered the magical call of China. It was a call that would always draw them back—just as it has drawn me back, and will do again.

Warm wishes,

Lucy Gordon

LUCY GORDON
And the Bride Wore Red

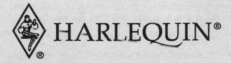

TORONTO • NEW YORK • LONDON
AMSTERDAM • PARIS • SYDNEY • HAMBURG
STOCKHOLM • ATHENS • TOKYO • MILAN • MADRID
PRAGUE • WARSAW • BUDAPEST • AUCKLAND

Recycling programs
for this product may
not exist in your area.

ISBN-13: 978-0-373-18484-2

AND THE BRIDE WORE RED

First North American Publication 2009.

Copyright © 2009 by Lucy Gordon.

www.eHarlequin.com

Printed in U.S.A.

Lucy Gordon cut her writing teeth on magazine journalism, interviewing many of the world's most interesting men, including Warren Beatty, Charlton Heston and Roger Moore. She also camped out with lions in Africa, and had many other unusual experiences, which have often provided the background for her books. Several years ago, while staying in Venice, she met a Venetian who proposed within two days. They have been married ever since. Naturally this has affected her writing, where romantic Italian men tend to feature strongly. Two of her books have won the Romance Writers of America RITA® Award.

You can visit her Web site at www.lucy-gordon.com.

*This book is dedicated to my friend Xin Ying,
who lives in Beijing and whose assistance with
Chinese social customs was invaluable.*

CHAPTER ONE

'OLIVIA, come quickly! There's been a terrible disaster!'

Olivia looked up from the school books she was marking to where Helma, the young teaching assistant, stood in the doorway. She was only mildly alarmed by the girl's agitated words. Helma had a wild sense of drama and 'a terrible disaster' might mean no more than the school cat making off with someone's lunch.

'It's Yen Dong!' Helma wailed.

Ten-year-old Dong was the brightest pupil in Olivia's class at the Chang-Ming School in Beijing. He was also the most mischievous, using his impish charm to evade retribution for his many escapades.

'What's he done now?' Olivia asked. 'Set a booby trap for the headmistress?'

'He's climbed a tree.'

'Again? Then he can just come down. It's almost time for afternoon lessons.'

'But he's ever so high and I don't think he can get down.'

Olivia hurried out into the garden that formed the school's playground and looked up. Sure enough, there was the little rascal, high on the tallest tree, looking cheerful even while hanging on for dear life.

'Can you climb down?' Olivia called.

He ventured a step, but his foot slid on the next branch and he backed off hastily.

'All right, not to worry,' Olivia said, trying to sound more confident than she felt. 'I need a ladder.'

One was fetched immediately, but to everyone's dismay it fell short of Dong by several feet.

'No problem,' Olivia sang out, setting her foot on the bottom rung.

Luckily she was wearing jeans, which made climbing easier, and reaching the top of the ladder wasn't too hard. But the next bit didn't look so easy. Taking a deep breath, she set her foot on a branch. It trembled but held, and she was emboldened to haul herself up. In another moment she had reached Dong, who gave her a beaming smile.

'It is very nice up here,' he said in careful, perfect English. 'I like climbing trees.'

Olivia looked at him askance. At any other time she would have been delighted with his command of her language. In the six months she'd spent teaching English at the Chang-Ming School, she'd found that Dong was the one who grasped everything first. She was proud of him, but right now she had other things to worry about.

'I like climbing trees too,' she said. 'But I also like getting down safely. So let's try to do that.'

She began to edge down, encouraging him to follow her so that he descended into the safety of her arms. One branch, then two, then three and finally, to her immense relief, the top rung of the ladder.

'Just a little further,' she said. 'Nearly there.'

But it was the ladder which failed them, sliding away from the tree suddenly and depositing them on the ground with a bump.

Olivia gasped as she felt the bark scrape painfully against her arm, but her real fear was for Dong.

'Are you hurt?' she asked worriedly.

He shook his head, refusing to be troubled by a few bruises, and bounced back onto his feet.

'I am well,' he pronounced.

Clearly this was true, but Olivia knew she had to be sure.

'I'm getting you to a doctor,' she said.

The headmistress had arrived on the scene in time to hear this. She was in her late forties with an air of common sense.

'That's a good idea,' she said. 'He seems fine,

but let's take no chances. There's a hospital ten minutes away. I'll call a taxi.'

A few minutes later they were on their way to the hospital. Olivia kept an anxious eye on Dong, but he was grinning, completely happy with the result of his escapade.

In the hospital someone showed them the way to the clinic, and they joined a short queue. A nurse gave Olivia some forms, and she filled them in while they waited to be seen.

A notice on the wall informed her that today's clinic was being taken by Dr Lang Mitchell. Briefly she wondered about that name; 'Mitchell' suggested that he might come from the West, but 'Lang' held a hint of Chinese.

After a few minutes the buzzer announced that the doctor was free, and they went in. Olivia saw a tall young man in his early thirties, with dark hair and eyes, and good-looking features that were mostly Western, yet with an intriguing hint of something else.

'What have you two been doing to yourselves?' he demanded, smiling and eyeing the state they were in.

'Miss Daley climbed a tree,' Dong said irrepressibly, 'and I went up to help her when she got stuck.'

Olivia looked aghast, which made Dr Mitchell grin in perfect comprehension.

'Perhaps it was the other way around?' he suggested.

'It certainly was,' Olivia declared, recovering her dignity. 'On the way down the ladder slipped, and we landed in a heap.'

He studied the forms. 'You are Miss Olivia Daley, a teacher at the Chang-Ming School?'

'That's right. Yen Dong is one of my pupils. I don't think he's hurt, but I have to be sure when I hand him back to his mother.'

'Of course. Let's have a look.'

After a thorough examination of Dong, he said, 'I agree that it doesn't look serious, but we'll have an X-ray just to be on the safe side. The nurse will take him.'

'Perhaps I should go too.'

But Dong shook his head, informing her that he was grown up and didn't need to be protected all the time. When he'd left with the nurse, the doctor switched to English to say, 'Let's see about your injuries.'

'Thank you. But I really don't need much done.'

Smiling, he said gently, 'Why don't you let me decide that?'

'Sorry,' she groaned. 'I just can't help it. My

aunt says if I'd shut up occasionally I might learn something.'

He smiled again but didn't answer directly. Then he frowned, saying, 'It might be worse than you think.'

Now she saw the true extent of the damage. The final slide against the bark of the tree had not merely scratched her flesh but torn the top of her sleeve so that it was barely hanging on.

'I'm afraid I'll need to remove your blouse,' Dr Mitchell said. 'The scratches seem to go further than your arm. Don't worry, a nurse will be present.'

He went to the door and called, 'Nurse.' A smiling young woman entered, removed Olivia's blouse gently and remained while he studied her abrasions. He eased her arm this way and that with movements that were as neat as they were skilful. His hands were large and comforting, both gentle and powerful together.

Disconcertingly she found herself becoming self-conscious. The blouse was high-necked and modest, even severe, as befitted a teacher, but beneath it she wore only a bra of fairly skimpy dimensions. She had breasts to be proud of, an unusual combination of dainty and luscious. Every bra she possessed had been designed to reveal them to one man, and although he was no longer part of her life she had never discarded them.

It had briefly crossed her mind to substitute underwear that was more sober and serious, but she'd rejected the thought as a kind of sacrilege. Now she wished she'd heeded it. Her generous curves were designed to be celebrated by a lover, not viewed clinically by a man who seemed not to notice that they were beautiful.

But that was as it should be, she reminded herself. The doctor was being splendidly professional, and deserved her respect for the scrupulous way he avoided touching her except when and where necessary. It was just disturbing that his restraint seemed to bring her physically alive in a way that only one man's touch had before.

He was cleaning her arm, swabbing it gently with cotton wool anointed with a healing spirit.

'This will sting a little,' he said. 'I'm sorry, are you all right?'

'Yes, I—'

'You jumped. I guess it stings more than I thought. Don't worry, I'll soon be finished.'

To her own dismay she'd sounded breathless. She hoped he didn't guess the reason, or notice the little pulse beating in her throat.

'Your diagnosis was quite correct,' he said after a while. 'Just a light dressing, I think. Nurse?'

The nurse did the necessary work, then helped

Olivia back on with her ruined blouse and departed. Dr Mitchell had retired behind his desk.

'How are you going to get home?' he asked, eyeing the tear.

'I look a bit disreputable, don't I?' she said with a laugh. 'But I've got this.' She took a light scarf from her bag and draped it over the spot. 'And I'll take a taxi. Just as soon as I know that Dong is all right.'

'Don't worry about him. I never saw such a healthy child.'

'I know,' she said with a shaky laugh. 'He's a rascal, I'm glad to say. No power on earth stops him getting up to mischief. He couldn't see the highest tree in the playground without wanting to climb it.'

'And that can be good,' Dr Mitchell said. 'Except that other people have to pick up the pieces, and often it is they who get hurt. I was much the same as a boy, and always in trouble for it. But I only recall my teachers reproving me, not risking their own safety to rescue me.'

'If he'd been seriously hurt, how could I have faced his mother?'

'But he isn't seriously hurt, because he had a soft landing on top of you.'

'Something like that,' she said ruefully. 'But nothing hurts me. I just bounce. And I should be getting him back to school soon, or he'll be late going home.'

'What about when you go home?' he asked. 'Is there anyone there to look after you?'

'No, I live alone, but I don't need anyone to look after me.'

He paused a moment before saying, 'Perhaps you shouldn't be too confident of that.'

'Why not?'

'It—can sometimes be dangerous.'

She wanted to ask him what he meant. The air was singing as though two conversations were happening together. Beneath the conventional words, he was speaking silently to a part of her that had never listened before, and it was vital to know more. She drew a breath, carefully framing a question…

'Here I am,' came a cheerful voice.

Suddenly she was back on earth, and there was Dong, trotting into the room, accompanied by the nurse with the X-ray.

'Excellent,' Dr Mitchell said in a voice that didn't sound quite natural to Olivia's ears. But nothing was natural any more.

As predicted, the X-ray showed no injury.

'Bring him back if he seems poorly,' Dr Mitchell told her, his tone normal again. 'But he won't.'

He showed her out and stood watching as she

vanished down the corridor and around the corner. Closing the door, he reached automatically for the buzzer, but stopped. He needed a moment to think before he saw another patient.

He went to stand at the window. Here, two floors high, there was a close-up view of the trees hung with cherry blossom; the promise of spring had been gloriously kept, and still lingered.

Here in China cherry blossom was a symbol of feminine beauty; seemingly delicate, yet laden with hope and promise. Now he saw that wherever he looked it was the same, as fresh new life returned after the cold, bringing hope and joy for those who were eager to embrace it.

On the surface nothing very much had happened. Olivia Daley was strong, independent, concerned not for herself but those in her care, much like the kind of woman a medical man met every day. It might only have been his imagination that beneath her composure was someone else— someone tense, vulnerable, needing help yet defiantly refusing to ask for it.

He could hear her again, insisting, *Nothing hurts me. I just bounce.*

He wondered if she truly believed herself so armoured to life. For himself, he didn't believe a word of it.

A few minutes they'd been together, that was

all. Yet he'd seen deep into her, and the sad emptiness he'd found there had almost overwhelmed him. He knew too that she'd been as disconcertingly alive to him as he had been to her.

He'd smothered the thought as unprofessional, but now it demanded his attention, and he yielded. She was different from other women. He had yet to discover exactly how different, and caution warned him not to try. Already he knew that he was going to ignore caution and follow the light that had mysteriously appeared on the road ahead.

It was a soft light, flickering and uncertain, promising everything and nothing. But he could no more deny it than he could deny his own self.

'Is everything all right?' asked the nurse from the doorway. 'You haven't buzzed.'

'I'm sorry,' he said with an effort. 'I just—got distracted.'

She smiled, following his gaze to the blossom-laden trees. 'The spring is beautiful, isn't it?'

'Yes,' he murmured. 'Beautiful.'

They arrived back at the school to find Mrs Yen, Dong's mother, waiting with a worried look that cleared as soon as she saw him waving eagerly.

'Perhaps you should take tomorrow off?' Mrs Wu, the headmistress, asked when they were finally alone.

'Thanks, but I won't need to.'

'Well, be sure. I don't want to lose one of my best teachers.'

They had been friends since the day Olivia had joined the school, charged with instructing the children in English. Now Mrs Wu fussed over her kindly until she went to collect her bicycle and rode it to her apartment, ten minutes away.

She had moved in six months ago, when she'd arrived to work in Beijing. Then she had been distraught, fleeing England, desperately glad to be embraced by a different culture which occupied her thoughts and gave her no time to brood. Now her surroundings and her new life were more familiar, but there were still new discoveries to be made, and she enjoyed every day.

She had a settled routine for when she arrived home. After a large cup of tea, she would switch on the computer and enter a programme that allowed her to make video contact with Aunt Norah, the elderly relative in England to whom she felt closest.

London was eight hours behind Beijing, which meant that back there it was the early hours of the morning, but she knew Norah would be ready, having set her alarm to be sure.

Yes, there she was, sitting up in bed, smiling and waving at the camera on top of her computer screen. Olivia waved back.

Norah was an old lady, a great-aunt rather than an aunt, but her eyes were as bright as they'd been her youth, and her vitality was undimmed. Olivia had always been close to her, turning to her wisdom and kindness as a refuge from the self-centred antics of the rest of her family.

'Sorry I'm late,' she said into the microphone. 'There was a bit of a kerfuffle at school today.'

She outlined the events of the afternoon, making light of them.

'And the doctor said you were all right?'

'He says I'm fine. I'll have an early night and be fit as a fiddle.'

'Are you going out with anyone?'

'You asked me that last night, and the night before. Honestly, Auntie, it's all you ever think of.'

'So I should hope. You're a pretty girl. You ought to be having a good time.'

'I'm having a wonderful time. And I do have dates. I just don't want to get serious. Now, tell me about yourself. Are you getting enough sleep?'

There was more in the query than just a desire to change the subject. Norah was in her seventies, and the only thing that had made Olivia hesitate about coming to China was the fear of possibly not seeing her again. But Norah had assured her that she was in the best of health and had urged her to go.

'Don't you dare turn down your chance because of me,' she'd insisted.

'I'm just trying to be sensible,' Olivia had protested mildly.

'*Sensible?* You've got the rest of your life for that sort of nonsense. Get out there, do things you've never done before, and forget that man who didn't deserve you anyway.'

Norah could never forgive the man who'd broken Olivia's heart.

'I'm sleeping fine,' Norah said now. 'I spent yesterday evening with your mother, listening to her complaining about her latest. That sent me right off to sleep.'

'I thought Guy was her ideal lover.'

'Not Guy, Freddy. She's finished with Guy, or he finished with her, one of the two. I can't keep up.'

Olivia sighed wryly. 'I'll call her and commiserate.'

'Not too much or you'll make her worse,' Norah said at once. 'She's a silly woman. I've always said so. Mind you, it's not all her fault. Her own mother has a lot to answer for. Fancy giving her a stupid name like Melisande! She was bound to see herself as a romantic heroine.'

'You mean,' Olivia said, 'that if Mum had been called something dull and sensible she wouldn't have eloped?'

'Probably not, although I think she'd have been self-centred whatever she was called. She's never thought of anyone but herself. She's certainly never thought of you, any more than your father has. Heaven alone knows what he's doing now, although I did hear a rumour that he's got some girl pregnant.'

'Again?'

'Yes, and he's going about preening as though he's the first man who's ever managed it. Forget him. The great fool isn't worth bothering with.'

Thus she dismissed her nephew—with some justice, as Olivia had to admit.

They chatted for a while longer before bidding each other an affectionate goodnight. Olivia delayed just long enough to make herself a basic meal, then fell thankfully into bed, ready to fall asleep at once.

Instead she lay awake, too restless for sleep. Mysteriously, Dr Mitchell had found his way into her thoughts, and she remembered him saying, *Other people have to pick up the pieces, and often it is they who get hurt.*

He'd given her a look full of wry kindness, as if guessing that she was often the person who had to come to the rescue—which was shrewd of him, she realised, because he'd been right.

As far back as she could remember she'd been

the rock of stability in her family. Her parents'
marriage had been a disaster. They'd married
young in a fever of romance, had quickly been disillusioned by prosaic reality and had headed for
divorce. Since then her mother had remarried and
divorced again before settling for lovers. Her
father had moved straight onto the lovers.

She herself had been passed from pillar to
post, depending on whichever of them had felt
she could be most useful. They had lavished
noisy affection on her without ever managing to
be convincing. Their birthday and Christmas
gifts had been expensive, but she'd realised early
on that they were aimed at scoring points off
each other.

'Let's see what your father thinks of that,' her
mother had said, proudly revealing a state-of-the-
art, top-of-the-range, laptop. But she'd been too
busy to come and see Olivia in the school play,
which would have meant far more.

The person who'd always come to school func-
tions was Norah, her father's aunt. When both her
parents had been busy, Olivia had gone to Norah
for long visits and found that here was someone
she could talk to. Norah had encouraged her to say
what she was thinking. She would argue, forcing
the girl to define her ideas then enlarge on them,
until Olivia had begun to realise that her own

thoughts were actually worth discussing—something she'd never discovered with her parents, who could talk only about themselves.

There'd always been a bedroom for her in Norah's home, and when she'd turned sixteen she'd moved into it full-time.

'How did that pair of adolescents you call parents react to the idea?' Norah demanded.

'I'm not sure they quite realise that I've gone,' Olivia said. 'He thinks I'm with her, she thinks I'm with him. Oh, what do they matter?'

It was possible to cope with her parents' selfish indifference because Norah's love was there like a rock. Even so, it was painful to discover yet again how little they really cared about her.

Eventually her mother asked, 'Will you be all right with Norah? She's a bit—you know—' she'd lowered her voice as though describing some great crime '—*fuddy-duddy.*'

It crossed Olivia's mind that 'fuddy-duddy' might be a welcome quality in a parent, but she said nothing. She'd learned discretion at an early age. She assured her mother that she would be fine, and the subject was allowed to die.

Before leaving, Melisande had one final request.

'Would you mind not calling me Mum when there are people around? It sounds so middle-aged, and I'm only thirty-one.'

Olivia frowned. 'Thirty-three, surely? Because I was born when—'

'Oh, darling, must you be so literal? I only *look* thirty-one. In fact, I've been told I look twenty-five. Surely you understand about artistic licence?'

'Of course,' Olivia agreed with a touch of bitterness that passed her mother by. 'And if I start claiming you as my mother it spoils the effect.'

'Exactly!' Melisande beamed, entirely missing the irony in her daughter's voice. 'You can call me Melly if you like.'

'Gosh, thanks, Mum.'

Her mother gave her a sharp look but didn't make the mistake of replying.

That evening, she told Norah, who was disgusted.

'Fuddy-duddy! She means I don't live my life at the mercy of every wind that blows.'

'She just thinks you know nothing about love,' Olivia pointed out.

When Norah didn't answer, she persisted, 'But she's wrong, isn't she? There's someone you never talk about.'

That was how she'd first heard about Edward, who'd died so long ago that nobody else remembered him, or the volcano he'd caused in the life of the girl who'd loved him. Norah told her only a little that night, but more later on, as Olivia grew old enough to understand.

Norah had been eighteen when she'd met Edward, a young army-officer, nineteen when they'd celebrated his promotion by becoming engaged, and twenty when he'd died, far away in another country. She had never loved another man.

The bleak simplicity of the story shocked Olivia. Later she learned to set it beside her own parents' superficial romances, and was equally appalled by both.

Had that lesson hovered somewhere in her mind when she too had fallen disastrously in love?

Looking back, she could see that her life-long cynicism about emotion, far from protecting her, had left her vulnerable. She'd determinedly avoided the youthful experiences on which most girls cut their romantic teeth, proud of the way her heart had never been broken because she'd never become involved. But it meant that she'd had no yardstick by which to judge Andy, no caution to warn her of signs that other women would have seen. Her capitulation to him had been total, joyful, and his betrayal had left her defenceless.

She'd fled, seeking a new life here in China, vowing never to make the same mistake again. From now on men would no longer exist. Neither would love, or anything that reminded her of 'the whole romantic nonsense' as she inwardly called it. And so she would be safe.

On that comforting thought, she fell asleep.

But tonight her sleep was mysteriously disturbed. Phantoms chased through her dreams, making her hot and cold by turns, causing her blood to race and her heart to pound. She awoke abruptly to find herself sitting up in bed, not knowing when it had happened, not knowing anything, except that suddenly there was no safety in all the world.

CHAPTER TWO

THE next day Olivia felt down from the moment she awoke. The sight of herself in the bathroom mirror was off-putting. Where was the vibrant young woman in her twenties with a slender figure, rich, honey-coloured hair and large blue eyes that could say so much?

'I don't think she ever really existed,' she informed her reflection gloomily. 'You're the reality.'

She wondered if she might still be in shock from her nasty fall, but dismissed that as just making excuses.

'I'm a hag,' she muttered. 'I look older than I am. I'm too thin, and my hair is just plain drab. I'll be going grey next.'

The woman in the mirror stared back, offering not a glimmer of sympathy. Normally Olivia wore her wavy hair long and bouncy but today she pulled it back into an efficient-looking bun. It suited her mood.

The day continued to be glum for no apparent reason. Her students were attentive and well-behaved, lunch was appetizing and her friends on the staff made kindly enquiries as to her health. Mrs Wu even tried to send her home.

'It's a reaction to that fall,' she said. 'Go home and rest.'

'Dong doesn't seem to need rest,' Olivia pointed out. 'I actually had to stop him trying to climb that tree again.'

'It's up to you,' the headmistress said sympathetically. 'But feel free to leave when you feel like it.'

She stuck it out to the end of the day, tired and grumpy, wanting to go home yet not looking forward to the empty apartment. Finally she delivered some papers to the headmistress and slipped out of the building by a side door, instead of the main entrance that she would normally have used. Then she stopped, arrested by the sight that met her eyes.

Dr Mitchell was there.

Now she knew that this moment was always meant to happen.

He was sitting on a low wall near the main entrance. Olivia paused for a moment just as he rose and began to pace restlessly and look at the main door as though expecting somebody to come through it. Occasionally he consulted his watch.

She backed off until she was in shadow under the trees, but still able to see him clearly. She realised that her view of him the day before had been constricted by the surroundings of his office. He was taller than she remembered, not muscular, but lean with a kind of casual elegance that yet hinted at tension and control.

Yesterday he'd been in command on his own territory. Now he was uncertain.

She began to walk towards him, calling, 'Can I help you?'

His face brightened at once, convincing her that she was the one he'd been awaiting. Mysteriously the day's cares began to fall away from her.

'I thought I'd drop in to see how my patients are,' he said, moving towards her.

'Do you always do follow-up visits from the clinic?'

He shook his head. His eyes were mischievous.

'Just this time,' he said.

'Thank you. Dong has already gone home, but he's fine.'

'But what about you? You were hurt as well.'

'It was only a few scratches, and I was cared for by an excellent doctor.'

He inclined his head in acknowledgement of her compliment, and said, 'Still, perhaps I should assure myself that you're really well.'

'Of course.' She stood back to let him enter the building, but he shook his head.

'I have a better idea. There's a little restaurant not far from here where we can talk in peace.'

His smile held a query, asking if she would go along with his strategy, and she hurried to reassure him, smiling in return and saying, 'What a lovely idea!'

'My car's just over there.'

To her pleasure he drove to a place that had a look that she thought of as traditionally Chinese. Much of Beijing had been rebuilt in a modern style, but she yearned for the old buildings with their ornate roofs turning up at the corners. Here she found them glowing with light from the coloured lamps outside.

The first restaurant they came to was full. So was the second.

'Perhaps we should try—'

He was interrupted by a cheerful cry. Turning, they saw a young man hailing him from a short distance away, and urgently pointing down a side street. He vanished without waiting to see if they followed him.

'We're caught,' her companion said ruefully. 'We'll have to go to the Dancing Dragon.'

'Isn't it any good?'

'It's the best—but I'll tell you later. Let's go.'

There was no mistaking the restaurant. Painted dragons swirled on the walls outside, their eyes alight with mischief. Inside was small and bright, bustling with life and packed.

'They don't have any tables free,' she murmured.

'Don't worry. They always keep one for me.'

Sure enough the man from the street reappeared, pointing the way to a corner and leading them to a small, discreet table tucked away almost out of sight. It had clearly been designed for lovers, and Lang must have thought so too, because he gave a hurried, embarrassed mutter, which Olivia just managed to decipher as, 'Do you have to be so obvious?'

'Why not?' the waiter asked, genuinely baffled. 'It's the table you always have.'

Olivia's lips twitched as she seated herself in the corner, but she controlled her amusement. Dr Mitchell was turning out to be more interesting than she would have guessed.

The restaurant was charming, the lanterns giving out a soft, red light, the walls covered in dragons. She regarded them in delight. Dragons had been part of her love affair with China ever since she'd discovered their real nature.

Raised in England, the only dragon she'd heard of had been the one slain by St George, a devil breathing fire and death, ravaging villages, demanding the sacrifice of innocent maidens, until the heroic knight George had overcome him and become the country's patron saint as a result.

In China it was different. Here the dragon had always been the harbinger of good luck, wealth, wisdom, a fine harvest. Delightful dragons popped up in every part of life. They danced at weddings, promenaded in parades, breathing their friendly fire and spreading happiness. They were all around her now.

Perhaps that was why she suddenly felt better than she'd done all day. There surely couldn't be any other reason.

Looking at a dragon painted onto a mirror, she caught sight of her own reflection and realised that her hair was still drawn back severely, which no longer felt right. With a swift movement she pulled at the pins until her tresses were freed, flowing lusciously again, in keeping with her lighter mood.

The dragon winked at her.

While Dr Mitchell was occupied with the waiter, Olivia remembered a duty that she must perform without delay. Whenever she was unable to make computer contact with Norah she always called to warn her so that the old woman wouldn't be left waiting in hope. Quickly she used her mobile phone and in a moment she heard Norah's voice.

'Just to let you know that I'm not at home tonight,' she said.

'Jolly good,' Norah said at once, as Olivia had known she would say. 'You should go out more often, not waste time talking to me.'

'But you know I love talking to you.'

'Yes, I do, but tonight you have more important things to think of. At least, I hope you have. Goodnight, darling.'

'Goodnight, my love,' Olivia said tenderly.

She hung up to find her companion regarding her with a little frown.

'Have I created a problem?' he asked delicately. 'Is there someone who—' he paused delicately '—would object to your being with me?'

'Oh, no! I was talking to my elderly aunt in England. There's nobody who can tell me who to be with.'

'I'm glad,' he said simply.

And she was glad too, for suddenly the shadows of the day had lifted.

'Dr Mitchell—'

'My name is Lang.'

'And mine is Olivia.'

The waiter appeared with tea, filling Olivia's cup, smiling with pleased surprise as she gave the traditional thank-you gesture of tapping three fingers on the table.

'Most Westerners don't know to do that,' Lang explained.

'It's the kind of thing I love,' she said. 'I love the story too—about the emperor who went to a tea-house incognito with some friends and told them not to prostrate themselves before him because it would give away his identity. So they tapped their fingers instead. I don't want to stand out. It's more fun fitting in.'

When the first dishes were laid out before them, including the rice, he observed her skill using chopsticks.

'You really know how to do that,' he observed as they started to eat. 'You must have been in China for some time.'

He spoke in Mandarin Chinese and she replied in the same language, glad to demonstrate that she was as expert as he.

'About six months,' she said. 'Before that I lived in England most of the time.'

'Most?'

'I've always travelled a lot to improve my languages. They were all I was ever good at, so I had to make the most of them.'

'How many languages do you speak?'

'French, German, Italian, Spanish…'

'Hey, I'm impressed. But why Chinese?'

'Pure show-off,' she chuckled. 'Everyone warned me it was difficult, so I did it for the fun of proving that I could. That showed 'em!'

'I'll bet it did,' he said admiringly, reverting to English. 'And I don't suppose you found it difficult at all.'

'Actually, I did, but I kept that to myself. You're the only person I've ever admitted that secret to.'

'And I promise not to reveal it,' he said solemnly. 'On pain of your never speaking to me again.'

She didn't have to ask what he meant by that. They both knew that the connection between them had been established in those few minutes of devastating consciousness in his surgery, and today he'd come looking for her because he had to.

Olivia thought back to last night, to the disturbance that had haunted her dreams, waking her and refusing to let her sleep again. Instinct told her that it had been the same with him.

They might spend no more than a few fleeting hours in each other's company, or they might travel a little distance along the road together. Neither could know. But they had to find out.

'So you came out here to improve your Chinese?' he asked in a tone that suggested there must be more to it.

'Partly, but I needed to get away from England for a while.'

He nodded, understanding at once. 'Was he a real louse?'

'I thought so at the time, but I think now I had

a lucky escape. He almost made me forget my prime directive. But when I discovered what a louse he really was, I realised that the prime directive had been right all the time.'

'Prime directive,' he mused, his eyes glinting with amusement. 'Now, let me see—what would that be? "Only learning matters." "Life can be reduced to graphs on a page." How am I doing?'

'You're part of the way there, but only part. Beware people, beware relationships—'

'Beware men!'

'Hey, you guessed.'

'It was obviously what you were building up to. Are we all condemned?'

'It's not that simple. I don't just condemn men, I blame women, as well.'

'Well, that seems to take care of the entire human race. Having disposed of the whole lot of them, let's go on eating.'

His wryly mocking tone made her laugh.

'My parents were both wild romantics,' she went on, 'and I can't tell you what a misfortune that is.'

'You don't need to. Romance isn't supposed to be for parents. Their job is to be severe and straight-laced so that their kids have a safety net for indulging in mad fantasies.'

'Right!' she said, relieved at his understanding. 'According to Aunt Norah it was love at first sight, then a whirlwind romance—moon rhyming with June. All that stuff.'

Lang regarded her curiously. Something edgy in the way she'd said *all that stuff* had alerted him.

'What happened?'

'She was seventeen, he was eighteen. Nobody took it seriously at first, just kids fooling around. But then they wanted to get married. The parents said no. He had to go to college. So she got pregnant—on purpose, Norah thinks. They ended up making a runaway marriage.'

'Wonderfully romantic,' Lang supplied. 'Until they came down to earth with a bump. He had to get a job, she found herself with a crying baby….'

'Apparently I cried more than most—for no reason, according to my mother.'

'But babies can sense things. You must have known instinctively that she was dissatisfied, wanting to go out and enjoy herself, and your father probably blamed her for his blighted career-prospects.'

She stared at him, awed by this insight.

'That's exactly how it was. At least, that's how Norah says it was. I don't remember, of course, except that I picked up the atmosphere without knowing why. There was lots of shouting and screaming.

'It got worse because they both started having

affairs. At last they divorced, and I found I didn't really have a home. I stayed with her, or with him, but I always felt like a guest. If there was a new girl-friend or new boyfriend I'd be in the way and I'd stay with Norah. Then the romance would break up and my mother would cry on my shoulder.'

'So you became *her* mother,' Lang observed.

'Yes, I suppose I did. And, if that was what romance did to you, I decided I didn't want it.'

'But wasn't there anyone else in your family to show you a more encouraging view of love? What about Norah?'

'She's the opposite to them. Her fiancé died years ago. There's been nobody else for her since, and she's always told me that she's perfectly content. She says once you've found the right man you can't replace him with anyone else.'

'Even when she's lost him?'

'But according to Norah she hasn't lost him. He loved her to the end of his life, so she feels that they still belong to each other.'

'And you disapprove?' he asked, frowning a little.

'It sounds charming, but it's really only words. The reality is that it's turned Norah's life into a desert that's lasted fifty years.'

'Perhaps it hasn't. Do you really know what's inside her heart? Perhaps it's given her a kind of fulfilment that we can't understand.'

'Of course you could be right, but if that's fulfilment…' She finished with a sigh. 'I just want more
from life than dreaming about a man who isn't there
any more. Or,' she added wryly, 'in my mother's
case, several men who aren't there any more.'

'But what about the louse? Didn't he change
your mind?'

For the first time he saw her disconcerted.

'I kind of lost the plot there,' she admitted. 'But
it sorted itself out. Never mind how. I'm wiser now.'

She spoke with a shrug and a cheerful smile, but
she had the feeling that he wasn't fooled. Some
instinct was telling him the things she wouldn't,
couldn't say.

She'd been dazzled by Andy from the first
moment. Handsome, charming, intelligent, he'd
singled her out, wooed her passionately and had
overturned all the fixed ideas of her life. For once
she'd understood Norah's aching fidelity to a dead
man. She'd even partly understood the way her
mother fell in love so often.

Then, just when she'd been ready to abandon
the prejudices of a lifetime, he'd announced that
he was engaged to marry someone else. He'd said
they'd had a wonderful few months together but
it was time to be realistic, wasn't it?

The lonely, anguished nights that had followed
had served to convince her that she'd been right

all the time. Love wasn't for her, or for anyone in their right mind. She couldn't speak of it, but there was no need. Lang's sympathetic silence told her that he understood.

'Tell me about you,' she hastened to say. 'You're English too, aren't you? What brought you out here?'

'I'm three-quarters English. The other quarter is Chinese.'

'Ah,' she said slowly.

'You guessed?'

'Not exactly. You sound English, but your features suggest otherwise. I don't know—there's something else…'

She gave up trying to explain. The 'something else' in his face seemed to come and go. One moment it almost defined him, the next it barely existed. It intrigued and tempted her with its hint of another, mysterious world.

'Something different—but it's not a matter of looks,' she finished, wishing she could find the right words.

He seemed satisfied and nodded.

'I know. That "something different" is inside, and it has always haunted me,' he said. 'I was born in London, and I grew up there, but I knew I didn't quite fit in with the others. My mother was English, my father was half-Chinese. He died soon after I was born. Later my mother married an Englishman with two children from a previous marriage.'

'Wicked stepfather?' Olivia enquired.

'No, nothing so dramatic. He was a decent guy. I got on well with him and his children, but I wasn't like them, and we all knew it.

'Luckily I had my grandmother, who'd left China to marry my grandfather. Her name was Lang Meihui before she married, and she was an astonishing woman. She knew nothing about England and couldn't speak the language. John Mitchell couldn't speak Chinese. But they managed to communicate and knew that they loved each other. He brought her home to London.'

'She must have found it really hard to cope,' Olivia mused.

'Yes, but I'll swear, nothing has ever defeated her in her life. She learned to speak English really well. She found a way to live in a country that probably felt like being on another planet, and she survived when her husband died ten years later, leaving her with a son to raise alone.

'He was called Lang too. She'd insisted on that. It was her way of keeping her Chinese family-name alive. When I was born she more or less bullied him into calling me Lang, as well. She told me later that she did it so that "we don't lose China."

'My father died when I was eight years old. When my mother remarried, Meihui moved into a little house in the next street so that she could be near me. She helped my mother with the children, the shopping, anything, but then she slipped away to her own home. And in time I began to follow her.'

He gave her a warm smile. 'So you see, I had a Norah too.'

'And you depended on her, just as I did on mine.'

'Yes, because she was the only one who could make me understand what was different about me. She taught me her language but, more than that, she showed me China.'

'She actually brought you here?'

'Only in my head, but if you could have seen the fireworks she set off in there.' He tapped his forehead. 'She used to take me out to visit London's Chinatown, especially on Chinese New Year. I thought I was in heaven—all that colour, the glittering lights and the music—'

'Oh, yes, I remember,' Olivia broke in eagerly. 'You saw it too?'

'Only once. My mother visited some friends who lived near there, and they took us out a couple of nights to see what was happening. It was like you said, brilliant and thrilling, but nobody could explain it to me. There was a lot of red, and they were supposed to be fighting somebody, but I couldn't tell who or what.'

'Some people say they're fighting the Nian,' Lang supplied. 'A mythical beast rather like a lion, who devours crops and children. So they put food out for him and let off firecrackers, because he's afraid of loud noises and also of the colour red. So you got lots of red and fireworks and lions dancing. What more could a child want?'

'Nothing,' Olivia said, remembering ecstatically. 'Oh, yes, it was gorgeous. So much better than the English New Year celebrations, which always seemed boringly sedate after that.'

'Me too. It was the one thing I refused ever to miss, and that drove my mother mad, because the date was always changing—late January, mid-February—always lasting fifteen days. Mum complained that she couldn't plan for anything, except that I'd be useless for fifteen days. I said, "Don't worry, Mum, I'm always useless".' He made a face. 'She didn't think that was at all funny.'

'Your grandmother sounds wonderful,' Olivia said sincerely.

'She was. She told me how everyone is born in the year of an animal—a sheep, an ox, a rat, a dragon. I longed to find I was born in the year of the dragon.'

'And were you?'

He made a face. 'No, I was born in the year of the rabbit. *Don't laugh!*'

'I'm not laughing,' she said, hastily controlling her mirth. 'In this country, the rabbit is calm and gentle, hard-working—'

'Dull and plodding,' he supplied. 'Dreary, conventional—'

'Observant, intelligent—'

'Boring.'

She chuckled. 'You're not boring, I promise.'

It was true. He delighted her, not with any flashy display of personality, but because his thoughts seemed to reach out and take hers by the hand in a way that, she now realized, Andy had never done.

He gave her a rueful grin.

'Thank you for those kind words, even if you had to scrape the bottom of the barrel to find them.'

'According to everything I've read, there's nothing wrong with being born in the year of the rabbit.'

'And you've obviously read a lot, so I guess you know your own year.' He saw her sheepish look and exclaimed, 'Oh, no, please don't tell me—!'

'I'm sorry, I really am.'

'The year of the dragon?'

'It not my fault,' she pleaded.

'You know what that means, don't you?' He

groaned. 'Dragons are free spirits, powerful, beautiful, fearless, they soar above convention, refusing to be bound by rules and regulations.'

'That's the theory, but I never felt it quite fitted me,' she said, laughing and trying to placate him. 'I don't see myself soaring.'

'But perhaps you don't know yourself too well,' he suggested. 'And you've yet to find the thing that will make you soar. Or the person,' he added.

The last words were spoken so quietly that she might have missed them, except that she was totally alive to him. She understood and was filled with sudden alarm. Things were happening that she'd sworn never to allow happen again.

She would leave right now and retreat into the old illusion of safety. All she had to do was rise, apologise and leave, trying to avoid his eyes that saw too much. It was simple, really.

But she didn't move, and she knew that she wasn't going to.

CHAPTER THREE

'THE trouble with soaring,' she murmured, 'is that you fall to earth.'

'Sometimes you do,' he said gently. 'But not always.'

'Not always,' she murmured. 'Perhaps.'

But it was too soon. Her nerve failed her and in her mind she crossed hastily to the cautious side of the road.

'What about your grandmother? What was her year?'

Tactfully he accepted her change of subject without demur.

'She was a dragon too,' he said. 'With her courage and sense of adventure she couldn't have been anything else—a real dragon lady. Everything she told me about this country seemed to bring me alive, until all I could think of was coming here one day.

'We planned how we'd make the trip together, but she became very ill. I'd qualified as a doctor by then, and I knew she wasn't going to recover, but she still talked as though it would happen soon.

'At last we had to face the truth. On her deathbed she said, "I so much wanted to be there with you." And I promised her that she would be.'

'And she has been, hasn't she?' Olivia asked, marvelling.

'Every step of the way,' he confirmed. 'Wherever I go, I remember what she told me. Her family welcomed me with open arms.'

'Did you find them easily?'

'Yes, because she'd stayed in touch. When I landed at Beijing Airport three years ago there were thirty people to welcome me. They recognised me at once from the pictures she'd sent them, and they all cheered.

'It's an enormous family. Not all of them live in Beijing, and many of those who lived further out had come in especially to see Meihui's grandson.'

'They weren't put off by your being three-quarters English?'

He laughed. 'I don't think they even see that part of me. I'm one of the Lang family. That's all that counts.'

'It was clever of your grandmother to name you and your father Lang,' Olivia mused. 'In England it's your first name, but here the family name comes first.'

'Yes, my uncles are Lang Hai and Lang Jing, my great uncle is Lang Tao, my cousin is Lang Dai, so I fitted in straight away.'

A sudden look of mischief crossed her face. 'Tell me something—have your stepbrothers given you any nephews and nieces?'

He looked puzzled. 'Three, but I don't see…'

'And I'll bet they call you Uncle Lang.'

'Yes, but—'

'And what do the children of the Lang family call you? It can't be Uncle Lang, because that would be nonsense to them. So I guess they must call you Uncle Mitch.'

A glazed look came into his eyes and he edged away from her with a nervous air that made her laugh.

'Are you a witch to have such second sight?' he demanded. 'Should I be scared?'

'Are you?' she teased.

'A bit. More than a bit, actually. How did you know that?'

'Logical deduction, my dear Watson. Second sight doesn't come into it.'

He could see that she was right, but it still left him with an enchanted feeling, as though she could divine what was hidden from others. A true 'dragon lady', he thought with delight, with magic arts to entice and dazzle a man.

'You're right about my grandmother,' he said. 'In her heart, she never really left China.'

'How did her relatives feel about her marrying an Englishman and leaving the country?'

'They were very supportive, because it's in the family tradition.'

'You all believe in marrying for love?'

'Much more than that. Marrying in the face of great difficulties, putting love first despite all obstacles. It goes back over two-thousand years.'

'Two thou…?' She laughed in astonishment. 'Are you nobility or something?'

'No, just ordinary people. Over the centuries my family has tilled the land, sold farm produce, perhaps made just enough money to start a little shop. We've been carpenters, wheelwrights, blacksmiths—but never noble, I promise you.'

The arrival of the waiter made him fall silent while plates were cleared away and the next course was served. It was fried pork-belly stewed in soy and wine, and Olivia's mouth watered at the prospect.

'We're also excellent cooks,' Lang observed, speaking very significantly.

'You mean…?'

'This was cooked by my cousin Lang Chao, and the guy who served it is his brother, Lang Wei. Later Wei's girlfriend, Suyin, will sing for us.'

'Your family own this restaurant?'

'That's why they virtually hijacked us. I wasn't planning to bring you here because I knew we'd be stared at—if you glance into the corner you'll see Wei sneaking a peek and thinking we can't see him—but they happened to spot me in the street, and after that we were lost.'

'We seem to be providing the entertainment,' she said, amused. 'Wei's enjoying a good laugh over there.'

'I'm going to strangle him when I get home,' Lang growled. 'This is why I didn't want them to see you because I knew they'd think— Well…'

'That you'd brought one of your numerous girl-friends here?' Olivia said.

She was teasing but the question was important.

'I occasionally bring a lady here to dine,' he conceded. 'Purely in a spirit of flirtation. Anything more serious, I wouldn't bring her here. Or at least,' he added, grinding his teeth and glaring at the unrepentant Wei, 'I'd *try* not to.'

'No problem.' Olivia chuckled. 'You tell him that he's completely wrong in what he's thinking, that we're just a pair of fellow professionals having a quiet meal for companionship. There's no more to it than that.'

'No more to it than that,' he echoed in a comically robotic voice.

'*Then* you can strangle him.'

'That sounds like a good idea. But what do I tell him when I take you out again?'

'Tell him to mind his own business?' she suggested vaguely.

'I can see you've never lived with a family like mine.'

'Wait a minute, you said when you "get home"? You don't live in the same house, do you?'

'Sometimes. I have a room there, but also a little place of my own near the hospital where I go if I've done a long stint at work and need to collapse. But if I want warmth, noise and cousins driving me crazy I go to the family home, so they tend to know what I do. But next time we'll avoid this place and have some privacy.'

'Look—'

'It's all right.' He held up a hand quickly. 'I don't mean to rush you. I know you haven't decided yet. But, when you do, let me know where you want to go.'

Her eyebrows rose at this quiet assurance but his smile disarmed her, making her complicit.

'I didn't finish telling you about our tradition,' he said.

'Yes, I'm curious. How did a family that had to work so hard come to put such a high value on romantic love? Surely it made more sense for a man to marry the girl whose father owned a strip of land next to his own?'

'Of course, and many marriages were made for such practical reasons. But the descendants of Jaio and Renshu always hoped for more.'

'Who were they?'

'They lived in the reign of the Emperor Qin, of whom I'm sure you've heard.'

She nodded. In reading about China, she'd learned about the time when it had been divided into many states. Qin Shi Huang, king of the state of Qin, had conquered the other states, unifying them into one gigantic country. Since Qin was pronounced 'chin' the country had come to be called China. Qin had proclaimed himself emperor, and on his death he'd been buried in a splendid mausoleum accompanied by any of his concubines who hadn't born him a child.

'One of those concubines was Jaio,' Lang told her now. 'She didn't want to die, and she was in love with Renshu, a young soldier who also loved her. Somehow he managed to rescue her, and they fled together. Of course, they had to spend the rest of their lives on the run, and they only had about five years before they were caught and killed. But by then they'd had a son, who was rescued and spirited away by Jaio's brother.

'Nobody heard anything for years, but when

the son was an old man he revealed the writings that Jaio and Renshu had left, in which they said that their love had been worth all the hardship. Of course, they had to be kept secret, but the family protected them and still has them to this day.

'Because of this the Langs have always cherished a belief in love that has seen them through many hard times. Often their neighbours have thought them mad for trusting in love when there were so many more *important* things in life, but they have clung to their ideals. It was that trust that made Meihui leave China and follow John Mitchell to England. And she never regretted it. She missed her homeland, but she always said that being with the man she loved mattered more than anything in life.'

Hearing these words, Olivia had a strange sense of familiarity. Then she realised that this was exactly what Norah would have said.

She sipped her wine, considering what she had just been told. On the surface it was a conventional legend—charming, a tad sentimental. What made it striking was that this serious man should speak as though it had a deep meaning for him.

'It's a lovely story,' she said wistfully. 'But did it really happen that way?'

'Why not?' he asked, giving her a quizzical smile.

She suppressed the instinct to say, *Because it's too absurdly romantic to be real*, and said, 'I only meant that two-thousand years is a terribly long time. So many things get lost in the mists, and you could never really know if they were true or not.'

'It's true if we want it to be,' he said simply. 'And we do.'

For a moment she almost queried who 'we' were, and then was glad she hadn't, because he added, 'All of us, the whole family—my aunts, great-aunts, my uncles, cousins—we all want it to be true. And so it is—for us.'

'That's a delightful idea,' she mused. 'But perhaps not very practical.'

'Ah, yes, I'd forgotten that you must always be practical and full of common sense,' he teased.

'There's a lot to be said for it,' she protested defensively.

'If you're a schoolteacher.'

'Doesn't a doctor need common sense, as well?'

'Often, but not always. Sometimes common sense is a much over-rated virtue.'

'And sometimes it can come to your rescue,' she said wryly.

She didn't realise that she'd spoken aloud until she saw him looking at her with a question in his eyes.

'Has it rescued you very often?' he asked gently.

'Now and then. It's nice to know I can always rely on it.'

'That's just what you can't do!' he said with sudden urgency. 'You must never rely completely on your head, because sooner or later it will always let you down.'

'And you think the heart doesn't?' she retorted with a touch of indignation. 'We're not all as lucky as Meihui.'

'Or Norah.'

'I'd hardly call her lucky.'

'I would,' he said at once. 'The man she loved died, but he didn't betray her. That makes her luckier than many women, and men too, who live for years with the shadows of failed love, bad memories, regrets. Or the others, who never dared risk love at all and have only thoughts of what might have been if only they'd had a little more courage.'

'That sounds very fine,' she said. 'But the fact is that most people are unlucky in love. Is there really much to choose between taking the risk and regretting it, and deciding not to take it at all?'

'And regretting that?'

'And living free,' she said defiantly. 'Free of regrets, free of pain—'

'Free of joy, free of the sense that life is worth living or ever has been?' he interrupted her firmly. 'Being free of pain can come at a heavy price.'

How had they strayed into this argument? she wondered. And why? The conversation was becoming dangerous, and she acted instinctively to get back into control.

'I see Wei coming towards us,' she said brightly.

If he noticed her abrupt change of subject he didn't say so. Instead he turned sardonic eyes on his cousin, who bustled forward eagerly, his gaze darting between the two of them.

'We'd like some fruit, please,' Lang said firmly. 'And then, *vanish*!'

Wei gave him a hurt look and departed with dignity. Lang ground his teeth.

'Sometimes I think I should have stayed well clear of my family,' he said.

Fruit was served, then tea, and then it was time for the entertainment. Two girls identically dressed in white-embroidered satin glided in. One, holding a small lute, seated herself, ready to play. The other stood beside her.

The lights dimmed except for the one on the performers. The first notes came from the lute and the singer began to make a soft crooning noise, full of a poignancy that was like joy and sadness combined. As Olivia listened an aching feeling came over her, as though the music had sprung all the locks by which she protected herself, leaving her open and defenceless as she had sworn never to be again.

The girl was singing in a soft voice:

'The trees were white with blossom.
We walked together beneath the falling petals.
But that is past and you are gone.
The trees do not blossom this year.
Aaaii-eeeii!'

That was how it had been; the trees hadn't blossomed this year and she knew they never would again. Andy had been an abject lesson in the need to stay detached. In future no man would hurt her like that because she wouldn't let it happen.

'The bridge still leads across the river,
Where we walked together.
But when I look down into the water,
Your face is not beside me.
Never again...'

Never again, she thought, not here or anywhere. She closed her eyes for a moment. But suddenly she opened them again, alerted by a touch on her cheek.

'Don't cry,' Lang said.

'I'm not crying,' she insisted.

For answer he showed her his fingertips, wet with her tears.

'Don't weep for him,' he said softly.

It would have been useless to utter another denial when he hadn't believed the first.

'I get sentimental sometimes.' She tried to laugh it away. 'But I'm really over him.'

In the dim light she could see Lang shake his head, smiling ruefully.

'Perhaps you belong together after all,' he said. Suddenly he reached into his pocket, took out his mobile phone and pushed it towards her, then he leaned close to murmur into her ear without disturbing the singer.

'Call him. Say that your quarrel was a mistake, and you love him still. Go on. Do it now.'

The dramatic gesture astonished and intrigued her. With a gasp of edgy laughter, she pushed the phone back to him.

'Why are you laughing?' he demanded.

'I was just picturing his face if he answered the phone and found himself talking to me. There was no quarrel. He left me for someone else. She had a lot of money, so he obviously did the right thing. I believe they're very happy. She bought him a posh car for a wedding present.'

'And that makes it the right thing?' he enquired.

'Of course.'

'So if a millionaire proposed you'd accept at once?'

'No way! He'd have to be a billionaire at least.'

'I see.' The words were grave but his lips were slightly quirked, as if he were asking who she thought she was fooling.

But he said nothing more. The music had ended. The singer bowed to the heartfelt applause and embarked on another song, slightly more cheerful. Lang turned his head towards the little stage, but reached back across the table to take hold of Olivia's hand, and kept it.

She found that her nostalgic sadness had vanished, overtaken by a subtle pleasure that seemed to infuse the whole evening. Everything was a part of it, including the man sitting opposite her, looking away, giving Olivia the chance to study him unobserved.

She could appreciate him like this. His regular features were enough to make him good-looking, but they also had a mobility that was constantly intriguing. His eyes could be bland and conventional, or wickedly knowing in a way that gave him a disconcerting charm. She wondered if there was anyone he regretted from his own past. A warm-natured man in his thirties, with a deep belief in the value of romantic love, had surely not reached this point without some sadness along the road.

She began to muse on the subject, wondering if there was a way to question him without revealing too much interest. There wasn't, of course, and an alarm bell sounded in her head. This was just the kind of atmosphere she'd learned to fear—seductive, romantic, lulling her senses and her mind in dangerous harmony.

It was time for common sense to take over. In a few minutes she would suggest that the evening should end soon, phrasing it carefully. She began to plan the words, even deciding what she would say when he protested.

Lang was beckoning to Wei, paying the bill, and ordering him to stop giggling and make himself scarce. Wei departed jauntily. Olivia took a deep breath to make her speech.

'We'd better go,' Lang said.

'Pardon?'

'We both have to work tomorrow, so I'll get you home quickly. I'm sorry to have kept you out so late.'

'Don't mention it,' she said faintly.

On the journey she wondered what was going to happen now. Lang had recognised that she wasn't ready for a decision, while subtly implying that he was attracted to her. He was charming and funny, with a quiet, gentle strength that appealed to her, perhaps because she could sense something quirky and irreverent beneath it.

A light-hearted flirtation could be agreeable, but if he wanted more, if he planned to end the evening in her arms—or even in her apartment—what then? A gentle let-down? How did you half-reject someone you more than half-liked? Again she began to think about what she would say to him.

When they arrived, he came with her to the apartment block.

'How far up are you?' he asked.

'Second floor.'

He rode up with her and came to her door.

'Lang?' she began uneasily.

'Yes?'

She lost her nerve. 'Would you care to come in for a drink?'

'I certainly want to come in, but not for a drink. Let's get inside and I'll explain, although I'm sure you know what the problem is.'

Once inside he took off his jacket and helped her off with hers.

'You'll need to remove your blouse as well,' he said, beginning to work on her buttons.

'Lang…'

He took no notice, opening the buttons one by one until he could remove the blouse, revealing her as he had the day before. She was astonished at his effrontery. Did he think he could simply undress her, seduce her, do as he liked with her?

'Now let me look at that arm,' he said.

'My arm?' she echoed, thunderstruck.

'That's why I came to find you tonight, isn't it?'

'Oh, yes—I remember.'

She had a horrible feeling that she sounded idiotic, but that was how she felt. He hadn't come here to seduce her, but to tend her. Her wild thoughts had been nonsense. She felt herself blushing from head to toe.

Then she thought she caught a gleam of mischief in his eyes, although it was gone before she could be certain.

With her blouse removed, he held her arm up, moving his head this way and that without appearing to notice anything but her injury. He had no eyes for the peachy, youthful glow of her skin, the way her waist narrowed and the lamp threw shadows between her breasts. It was almost insulting.

'This is the last time it will need covering,' he said. 'It's healing nicely.'

He'd brought a small bag in with him, and from it he took replacement dressings. He covered the grazes lightly, and fixed everything in place.

'Now get a good night's sleep,' he instructed.

Then he was heading out of the apartment, without having touched her, except as a doctor.

'Wait,' she said desperately. 'What did you mean about "the problem"?'

He paused in the doorway.

'The problem,' he said, 'is that you're still my patient. Later…'

'Later?'

His gaze moved over her slowly, lingering just a little on the beauty he had so dutifully ignored.

'Later you won't be. Goodnight.'

The school term was nearly over. Olivia was busy writing reports, talking to parents and consulting with the headmistress, who looked in on her on the penultimate day.

'I'm just making plans for next year,' she said cheerfully. 'I'm so glad you're staying.'

'Staying?' Olivia echoed vaguely.

'You originally came for six months, but when I asked if you were going to stay on you said you would. Don't you remember?'

'Oh, yes—yes.'

'You really sound in need of a holiday,' Mrs Wu said kindly.

'It's just that I've been wondering if I should go home.'

'But you can do that and still come back next term. From all you've told me about Norah, she wants you to stay here and spread your wings. I hope you come back. You're doing such a good job. But you've got my number if you have a last-minute change of mind.'

Olivia went home, thoughtful. Everything that had seemed simple only a short while ago had suddenly become complicated.

It was true that Norah showed no sign of wanting her early return. Only last night she'd been at her most lively, talking furiously about Melisande's latest lover.

'You mean, Freddy?' Olivia had queried.

'No. Freddy's finished since she caught him sleeping with a pole dancer. It's your father.'

'Mum and Dad? What are they playing at?'

'I gather he went to see her, seeking solace from a broken heart.'

'I thought you said he'd made some girl pregnant.'

'He thought he had, but apparently it's not his, so he went to cry on your mother's shoulder because, and I quote, "she's the only one who understands".'

'Give me patience!'

'That's what I said. Anyway, it seems that they looked at each other across the barrier of years, heart spoke to heart as though time and distance had never been…'

'What?'

'I told her to get out before she made me ill. It's just her putting herself centre-stage again, as always.'

Olivia had had to agree. She'd seen, and suffered from, enough of her parents' selfish grand-standing to dismiss this great romance as just another show in the spotlight.

You could say much the same of all great romances, she thought. Her father would let her mother down again, because that was what men did. It was what Andy had done. And who cared if Lang called her or not?

Several days had passed since their last meeting. After talking so significantly he had fallen silent, and with every passing hour Olivia had condemned herself more angrily as a fool.

It wasn't as if she hadn't been warned, she told herself crossly. When Andy had appeared in her life, she'd abandoned the caution so carefully built up over a lifetime because she'd convinced herself that *this* man was different.

But no man was different, as she'd learned in anguish and bitterness. She'd vowed 'never again', but then she'd been tricked into ignoring those resolutions because Lang had charmed her.

No, it was more than charm, she admitted. It was the sense of quiet understanding, the feeling that his mind and heart were open to hers, and that she would find in him generosity and understanding.

Heart spoke to heart as though time and distance had never been.

Her mother's melodramatic words shrieked a

warning in her head. She and Lang had met only a couple of times, and came from different worlds, yet time and distance did not exist, hadn't existed between them from the first moment.

Which meant that she would fight him all the harder. If she made the foolish mistake of falling in love with Lang, the misery would be far greater than before.

It was useful that he'd shown his true colours in time to prevent a disaster. She repeated that to herself several times.

But no way would she stay here, pining. If she didn't return to England, she'd go somewhere else. She got a brochure advertising cruises along the great Yangtze River and booked herself a cabin. She would board the boat at Chongqing, leave it at Yichang and travel on to Shanghai. After that, who could tell where she would travel? And what did it matter? What did anything matter as long as she had no time to think?

CHAPTER FOUR

ON THE last day of term Olivia counted the minutes until it was time to go. Just a little longer and she need never think of Lang again. *Concentrate on the Yangtze. Think of Shanghai.*

The last pupil had gone home. She was gathering up her things when a buzz made her look at her mobile phone, where there was a text: *I'm outside.*

For a brief moment her heart leapt, then indignation took over. Cheek! Like he only had to announce his presence and she must jump.

She texted back: *I'm busy.*

The reply came at once: *I'll wait.*

Mrs Wu looked in to say goodbye and they left the building together.

'Have a good holiday,' she said. 'And please dispose of that young man hanging around the gate. Loiterers are bad for the school's reputation.'

'He's nothing to do with me.'

'Of course he isn't. That's why his eyes are fixed on you. Goodbye for now.'

Lang was leaning against the wall as though there was all the time in the world, which did nothing to improve her mood. She advanced on him in a confrontational mood, and thrust out her arm, from which she'd removed the dressing.

'Just a few scratches and healing nicely, thank you,' she said in a formal voice.

'You don't know how glad I am to hear that.'

'And the headmistress says I'm to get rid of you. You're giving the place a bad name.'

'In that case, let's go.'

'I don't think—'

'Let's not waste any more time.' He already had hold of her arm and was ushering her into his car, which he started up quickly, as though afraid to give her time to think.

Had he known it, she was beyond coherent thought, beyond anything but wild emotion. He hadn't abandoned her, hadn't turned away, leaving her desolate. He had come for her because he could no more escape the bonds tightening around them than she could.

She knew she should try to control the heady, idiotic feeling that pervaded her. It was too much like joy: terrifying, threatening, destructive, glorious joy.

At last she managed to speak and ask where they were going. At least, that was what she thought she'd asked. She was too confused to be sure.

'I'm taking you somewhere that will help you get over being grumpy,' he replied.

'I'm not grumpy.'

'Yes you are. When you saw me outside the school, you glared hard enough to terrify the devil.'

'Well, it was very inconsiderate of you to arrive in the last five minutes.'

'You couldn't possibly have been hoping to see me earlier?'

'Certainly not. You just disrupted my schedule. I like things done in the proper order.'

'Just as I said, grumpy. Meihui used to have a way of dealing with my bad moods—several ways, actually—but this was our favourite one.'

More than that he would not say, but he drove for half an hour in silence, glad of the chance to say nothing and collect his thoughts. Unusually for him, they were chaotic.

After their last meeting he'd resolved not to approach Olivia again, at least, not soon. He was an ambitious man, and his career was beginning to look promising. He needed no distractions, and the sensible course would be to let the summer vacation pass before they met again. The passage of a little time would put him in control of himself again.

It had all been very simple. Until today.

The summer break from his job had already started, which was unlucky, because if he'd been at work he couldn't have yielded to temptation. As it was, the realisation that she would be leaving any minute had galvanised him. Suddenly his resolutions were rubbish, his strength of will non-existent. He'd barely made it to the school in time.

Now he was calling himself names, of which 'weakling' was the kindest. But the abusive voice was bawling only from the back of his head; the front was full of relief that he'd made it in time.

There was another voice too, not yelling, but muttering. This was his conscience, warning him that there was something he must confess to her without delay. He wasn't sure what her reaction would be. That troubled him more than anything.

'Here we are,' he said, drawing up outside a huge gate.

'You've brought me to a zoo?' she said, astounded.

'Meihui said nobody could stay cross in a zoo. So let's go in.'

He was right, after only a few minutes of wandering around the animals, her spirits lightened. Who cared about anything else when there were lions to be viewed, bears to watch, exotic birds?

Lang was like no other man. When was the last time anyone had taken her to a place like this? she wondered as they gazed at the giant pandas.

'I've never seen anything so beautiful,' she murmured.

'They're magnificent, aren't they?' he agreed warmly.

'But how do you tell one from the other? Pandas all look exactly alike.'

'The one over there on her own in the tree is the female. Earlier this year she was in heat for a couple of days, and had all the males swooning after her. Now she's safely pregnant, and they can go and jump in the lake for all she cares.'

'I wonder which male she favoured.'

'The highest ranking one. He proved his status by knocking seven bells out of the competition.'

'Very sensible,' Olivia said. 'None of that sentimental nonsense. If ever I'm reborn, I shall come back as a panda.'

He laughed but said, 'Why do you have to be so severe?'

'I'm not severe.'

'You are from where I'm standing.'

'Oh, I see, a *male* version of severe—meaning a woman who doesn't collapse in a sentimental heap at the mention of *lurve*.' She gave the word a satirical inflection that made him wince. '*That* kind of severe.'

'You put it very crudely,' he complained.

'The truth is usually crude, and definitely

unromantic. Like life. We just have to face up to it.'

She was saying the first thing that came into her head and enjoying the sight of his face. For once the confident Dr Mitchell was struggling for words, and that was fun.

'Why are you so determined not to believe in love?' he asked. 'I know you had a bad experience, but so have most people, and they don't abandon hope. I didn't give up when Becky Renton told me it was all over.'

'Oh, yes? And I'll bet the two of you were about twelve when that happened.'

He grinned. 'A little older than that, but you've got the right idea.'

She wondered if this handsome, assured man had ever been dumped in his life. Not by anyone he really cared about, she would have bet on it.

'Joking apart,' he resumed, 'people really do do things for love. I know you don't believe it, but it's true.'

'If you're talking about your romantic ancestors, allow me to point out that there's no reason to believe that Jaio was ever in love. They were going to lock her in the tomb and Renshu offered escape. She might simply have thought that going with him was better than dying.'

'But what about him? He must have loved her a lot because he sacrificed everything to be with her.' Lang added provocatively, 'Perhaps it really means that a man can love more deeply than a woman. It could even be doubted that women know how to love at all. They believe in logic rather than sentiment—like pandas.'

Olivia eyed him askance. 'Did you say that just to be annoying?'

'No, I think it's an interesting theory.' Catching her expression, he couldn't resist adding, 'But I must admit I also enjoy annoying you.'

'You'll go too far.'

'I hope so. Better too far than not far enough.'

His grin was her undoing, leaving her no choice but to smile back.

'Let's find the snack bar,' he said, slipping an arm around her shoulders.

As they sat down over coffee, Lang suddenly said, 'I hope you can forgive my clumsiness.'

'About what?'

'That remark about choosing a mate through logic rather than sentiment. It's exactly what your louse boyfriend did, isn't it? I'm sorry. I didn't mean to hurt you.'

'You didn't,' she said, realising that it was true. She hadn't even thought about Andy. Nor, now she thought of it, had she ever enjoyed such a day as this, strolling calmly through pleasant gardens, teasing and testing each other.

There had been no jokes with Andy, only passion and violent emotion, which at the time she'd thought was enough. But with Lang she was discovering how emotion could be tempered with humour. He was a patient man who knew when to back off. It made him a restful companion, as well as an exciting one, and that too was a new pleasure.

'I've dismissed Andy from my mind,' she told him, adding with a flourish, 'It was the common sense thing to do.'

'That easy, huh?'

'Of course. Logic over sentiment any day. I reckon the female panda knows exactly what she's doing.'

'Then I'm glad I'm not a panda,' he said, matching her flourish with one of his own.

Before they left the zoo he took her to the gift shop and bought her a small soft toy in the shape of a panda.

'She's a female,' he declared.

'How can you tell?'

'Because that's what I want her to be,' he said, as though explaining the obvious. 'Her name is Ming Zhi. It means wise.' His eyes gleamed with mischief. 'It was the nearest I could get to logic and common sense.'

'Then she and I will get on very well,' Olivia declared, taking the delightful creature and rubbing her face against its soft black-and-white fur. 'If I forget what's important, she's bound to remind me.'

'To the victory of logic,' he proclaimed.

'Every time.'

'Let's go and have some supper.'

They found a small, old-fashioned restaurant.

'Why were you in such a bad mood when we met earlier?' he asked when they were settled. 'Is it me you're annoyed with?'

'No, my parents. According to Norah, they've rediscovered each other, acting like love's young dream.'

'Which could be charming.'

'If it was anyone else, it could, but this pair of raging play-actors are heading for disaster.'

'Don't be so sure,' Lang said. 'Maybe they just married too young and were always meant to find each other again.'

She gave him a look.

'Maybe not,' he said hastily.

'In the end it'll collapse in lies, as it did the first time.' Olivia sighed. 'And there's nothing so fatal as deception.'

'Sometimes a deception can be fairly innocent,' Lang observed casually.

'But it's always destructive,' she insisted. 'Once you know he hasn't been straight with you, it's over, because—I don't know. I'm going to eat.'

Concentrating on her chopsticks, she didn't see the uncomfortable look that came over Lang's face.

'This food is nice,' she said after a while. 'But not as nice as at the Dancing Dragon.'

To her surprise he didn't respond to the compliment. He seemed sunk in thought, and strangely uneasy.

'Is everything all right?' she asked.

'No,' he said with an effort. 'There's something I have to tell you.'

There was a heaviness in his voice that filled Olivia with foreboding.

'I must admit that I've been putting this moment off,' Lang continued awkwardly. 'I was afraid it would make you think badly of me. I know I've done wrong, but I didn't want to risk not seeing you again.'

Now she knew what he was trying to say: he had a wife.

Impossible. In that case he would never have taken her to the Dancing Dragon where they would be seen by his family. But perhaps the family's attitude had simply been curiosity that their foreign relative was playing around. She tried to recall exactly what they had said, and couldn't.

'Will you promise to let me finish explaining before you condemn me?' he asked.

By ill luck, Andy had said much the same thing: 'If only you'd let me explain properly, it really wasn't my fault…'

A chill settled over her heart.

'Go on then,' she said. 'Tell me the worst.'

Lang took a deep breath and seemed to struggle for words.

'The fact is—' he began, stopped then started again. 'When we met—' He was floundering.

'Look,' she said edgily, 'why don't we just skip it and go home?'

'Don't you want to know what I have to say?'

'I probably already know what you're going to say,' she observed with a faint, mirthless laugh.

'You guessed? I don't see how you could have done.'

'Let's say I have a nose for some things. Call it my cynical nature.'

'I don't think you're as cynical as you try to pretend.'

Her temper flared. 'And I don't think you know anything about me.'

He stared. 'All right, don't jump on me. I'm harmless, I swear it. I'll believe that you're anything you say—hard, cynical, unfeeling…'

'Ruthless, unforgiving, cold-hearted,' she supplied. 'I'm glad you understand.'

'I wish you hadn't said unforgiving,' he observed gloomily.

'Well, I did say it. I never give second chances. Now, if we've got that settled, what were you going to confess? Something unforgivable, obviously.'

'Well, you might think so.'

Her dismay increased. 'All right. I'm listening.'

'It's like this. When we met in that clinic—I wouldn't normally be there. I work in another part of the hospital, and I'd just started a vacation. But a friend who does work in the clinic got a stomach upset and had to take time off. They were short staffed, so I filled in.'

'But what's so terrible about that?' she asked, trying to think straight through the confusion of reactions storming through her.

'The thing is, he was back next morning. I did try to persuade him that he needed another day off, but he got an attack of heroics and insisted on returning.' Lang sighed and added distractedly, 'A man can't trust his friends for anything, not even to be ill when he needs them to be.'

'What on earth are you—?'

'So when I came to see you next day I wasn't working in the clinic any more, and strictly speaking you were no longer my patient.'

Olivia stared at him in mounting disbelief. 'Are you saying...?'

'That I lied to you,' he said mournfully. 'I approached you under false pretences, claiming that you were my patient when you no longer were. I deceived you.'

Olivia met his eyes and drew a quick breath at what she saw there, a look of suspiciously bland innocence that masked something far from innocent. This man wasn't worried about being in trouble. He was inviting her into a conspiracy.

'You're overdoing it,' she said wryly.

'No, honestly! On the pretext of medical privilege, I gained access to your body.'

'To my—? Oh, yes, you saw my bare arm, didn't you?' she said sardonically. 'How could I have forgotten that? Shocking!'

'It was a little more than your arm,' he reminded her. 'If you want to report me to the medical authorities, well, I'll just have to accept it, won't I?'

'And if I kicked your shins you'd just have to accept that, wouldn't you?' she said sweetly.

'It would be my just deserts.'

'Don't get me started on your just deserts or we'll be here all night.'

'Would we? Tell me more.'

'Let's just say that you're a devious, treacherous— I can't think of anything bad enough.'

'I'll wait while you think of something. After all, it was shocking behaviour on my part.'

'I didn't mean that. I meant just now, making me think—'

'What?'

She pulled herself together. 'Making me think it was something really serious, instead of just fooling.'

She could barely speak for the confusion of relief and fear that warred in her: relief that he was a free man, fear that it mattered so much. She tried to bring herself under control lest he guess the truth.

Or did he already know? He was watching her intently but cautiously, as though trying to discover something that was important to him.

'I wanted to see you again,' he said simply. 'And that was the best excuse I could find.'

The storm died down. The relief was still there, but now tinged with laughter. The world was bright.

'Well, I guess I'm glad you thought of something,' she admitted.

He took her hand. 'So am I.'

'I'm still annoyed with you, but I forgive you—on a purely temporary basis.'

'That's all I ask.'

'So what is your job in the hospital?'

Lang shrugged. 'I fill in a lot, do the stuff

nobody else wants.' He squeezed her hand gently. 'Sometimes I get a good day.'

He didn't pursue the subject and she was glad. The attraction between them was growing slowly, delicately, and she liked it that way. Any sudden movements might be fatal.

He was looking down at her hand, rubbing his fingers against it softly, and she had the feeling that he was uneasy again.

'What is it?' she asked. 'What terrible crime do you have to admit now?'

'We-ell…'

'Be brave. It can't be worse than you've already confessed.'

'The fact is there have been some repercussions to the other night. Wei, the great blabbermouth, went home and sounded off to my family, telling them all about you.'

'But he doesn't know anything about me— unless, of course, you've told him, which would be another abuse of medical privilege.' She considered him, her head on one side. 'You really are proving to be a disreputable character. Interesting, but disreputable.'

'This time I plead not guilty. Anything I know about you—which is frustratingly little—I keep firmly to myself. Wei's method is to invent what he doesn't know. The family's curiosity is aroused, and now there'll be no peace until I take you home for dinner.'

'Let me get this straight. You want to take me home just to save yourself from nagging?'

'That's about the size of it.'

'It's got nothing to do with wanting my company?'

'Certainly not,' he said in a shocked voice.

'It wouldn't mean that you were glad to be seen with me, liked me for myself, and maybe, I don't know…?'

'Maybe thought you were the prettiest girl I'd ever seen and the nicest I'd ever been out with?' he supplied helpfully. 'No, nothing like that. Don't worry.'

'You relieve my mind,' she said gravely.

He raised her hand and brushed his cheek against the back of her fingers.

'I think we should stay level-headed,' he said. 'I wouldn't want to offend you by indulging in the kind of sentimental behaviour I know you despise.'

'That's thoughtful of you. On the other hand, your family are going to expect us to seem at ease with each other. We mustn't disappoint them by being too distant.'

He nodded as though giving this judicious consideration.

'True. We need to get it just right.'

Before she knew what he meant to do, he leaned across the table and laid his lips softly against hers.

It was the briefest of contacts. No sooner was his mouth there than it was gone again. It might never have happened, yet it went through her like lightning, making nonsense of logic and control, leaving her changed and the world a different place.

She tried to smile with careless unconcern, but her heart was thumping, and there was no way she could seem indifferent. To hide her confusion she looked down, but when she raised her head again everything was more confusing, because now she could see that Lang was startled too.

'That should be about right,' she managed to say.

She was lying. It wasn't about right, it wasn't nearly enough. One whispering touch and something inside her had sprung to life, making her tingle with frustration. She wanted more, and so did he. His expression had told her that. Yet here they were, two well-behaved dolls, bound and gagged by the constraints that they had set themselves. Only a moment ago it had seemed amusing.

'So what can I tell the family?' he asked, and she wondered if she only imagined that his voice was shaking.

'I'd be delighted to accept their kind invitation when I return from my travels.'

'You're going away? When? Where?'

'I'm taking a cruise down the Yangtze.'

'But not tomorrow?'

'No, in three days but—'

'Fine, that gives us plenty of time.' He whipped out his mobile phone and dialled hurriedly. 'Better do this before you can change your mind. You're a very confusing person. I never know where I am with you.'

After the days she'd spent longing to hear from him—which she now admitted to herself she had—this left her speechless with indignation. While she was still trying to think of something bad enough to call him, he began talking into the phone.

'Hallo, Aunt Biyu? Olivia says she'd be delighted. Yes, yes.' He looked back at Olivia. 'Do you like dumplings?'

'I love them,' she said promptly.

'She loves them, Aunt Biyu— What's that? All right, I'll ask her. Do you prefer meat or vegetables?'

'I'm happy with either.'

'She's happy with either. Oh, yes, that sounds nice.' To Olivia he said, 'Shrimp and bamboo, OK?'

'Yes, splendid,' she said, slightly confused.

Lang turned back to the phone. 'Olivia is thrilled with shrimp and bamboo. Tomorrow evening?' He raised an eyebrow and Olivia nodded. 'Tomorrow's fine. Goodnight.'

He hung up. 'Aunt Biyu is married to Uncle Hai. She's preparing you the best shrimp and bamboo you ever tasted, and the whole family is helping. You're a very important guest.'

She knew enough about Chinese culture to recognise that this was true. In the old days of poverty, dumplings had been the staple food, and had subsequently acquired a place of honour. To lay out a banquet of dumplings for a guest was to pay a compliment.

She began to wonder exactly what Lang had told them. As he drove her home later, he was smiling.

At her apartment block he saw her to the main front door, but didn't try to come any further.

'I'll collect you at six o'clock tomorrow evening,' he said.

'Yes. Goodnight.'

'Goodnight.'

He hesitated for a moment, then leaned forward suddenly and gave her the briefest possible kiss before hurrying away.

Olivia was thoughtful as she entered her apartment. Nothing in the world seemed clear or simple, and it was because of Lang, a man she'd met only three times.

Reaching into her bag, she felt something soft and silky, and realised that she'd forgotten all about Ming Zhi. The little panda regarded her severely, reminding her that she was a sensible woman who had renounced love in favour of logic.

'Oh, shut up!' Olivia said, tossing her onto the bed. 'I don't care if he did give you to me. You're a pain in the whatsit. And so is he.'

That night she slept with Ming Zhi in the crook of her arm.

CHAPTER FIVE

NEXT morning she went online to Norah and was rewarded by the sight of the old woman waving and smiling at the camera.

'So, what are you going to do with your holidays?' she asked. 'Did you book that cruise?'

'Yes, I'll be off in a few days.'

'And?' Norah probed, for Olivia's tone clearly hinted at something else.

'I've met this madman…'

She tried to describe Lang. It wasn't easy, for he seemed to elude her even as she spoke. Calling him a madman was the truth, but far from the whole truth, and she was still discovering the rest.

'He can make me laugh,' she said.

'That's always a good beginning.'

'And he gave me this.' She held up Ming Zhi. 'When we went to the zoo.'

'Now, that looks like getting serious. When are you seeing him again?'

'This evening. He's taking me to have dinner with his family.'

'Already? My dear, he's moving very fast.'

'No, it's not like that. One of his relatives saw us together and the family got curious. He's only taking me home to shut them up.'

'Is he a wimp, that he can't stand up to them?'

'No, he's not a wimp,' Olivia said, smiling and remembering how Lang gave the impression of being quietly in command, except when he was being jokingly deferential to make her laugh. 'He pretends to be sometimes, but that's just his way of catching me off-guard.'

'And does he often succeed?'

'Yes,' Olivia admitted wryly. 'He does.'

'Then he must be a very clever man indeed. I look forward to meeting him.'

'Norah, please! You're going much too fast. Lang and I have only met a few times. I'm not looking for anything serious. We'll enjoy a brief relationship and then I'll come home. In fact—'

'Don't you dare start that again. You stay where you are, and *live* your life. Don't throw it away.'

'All right, I promise,' Olivia said. She was slightly startled by Norah's intensity; a kind of anguish almost seemed to possess her.

'You spend as much time with Lang as you can. He sounds nice. Is he good-looking?'

'Yes, he's good-looking?'

'*Really* good-looking?'

'Well…'

'On a scale of one to ten?'

'Seven. Oh, all right—eight.'

'Jolly good,' Norah said robustly. 'Now, go and buy a really nice, new dress. Splash out, do you hear?'

'Yes, Aunt,' Olivia said meekly, and they laughed together.

After a hasty breakfast she headed out to the shops, meaning to choose something from the Western fashions that were now available in Beijing. But before long her eye fell on a *cheongsam*, the traditional Chinese dress that was so flattering to a woman with a good figure. The neckline came modestly up to the throat, and there was a high-standing collar, but it was also figure-hugging, outlining her tiny waist, flared hips and delicately rounded breasts in a way that left no doubt that her shape was perfect.

It was heavily embroidered and made of the highest-quality silk, at a price that made her hesitate for half a second. But when she tried it on and saw what it did for her she knew she was lost. When she combined it with the finest heels she dared to wear, the effect was stunning.

She wondered if Lang would think so. Would he compliment her on her appearance?

He did not. Calling for her punctually at six, he handed her into the car without a word. But she'd seen the way his eyes had lingered on the swell of her breasts, so perfectly emphasised by the clinging material, and she knew he had remembered their first meeting. His expression told her all she wanted to know.

She settled down to enjoy herself. They were headed for the *hutongs*; she'd always been fascinated by these streets that had surrounded the Forbidden City for hundreds of years. A plentiful water supply had dictated the location, and the *hutongs* had always flourished, colourful places full of life and industry. Shops sprung up, especially butchers, bakers, fishmongers and anything selling domestic necessities. Change came and went. Other parts of the city had become wealthier, more fashionable, but the *hutongs*' vibrant character had ensured their survival.

Olivia had sometimes shopped there. Now for the first time she would see the personal life that lay behind the little stores. A *hutong* was a street formed by lines of quadrangles, called *siheyuans*, each *siheyuan* consisting of four houses placed at right angles to each other. Here large families could live with the privacy of their own home, yet with their relatives always within calling distance.

As they drove there, Lang described his family's *siheyuan*.

'The north house belongs to Grandfather Tao. He's the centre of the family. Meihui was his kid sister and he remembers her as if it were yesterday. He says I remind him of her, but that's just affection, because I don't really look like her at all. Uncle Jing and his wife also live there, with their four children.

'One of the side houses is occupied by Uncle Hai, his wife and their two younger children. The one opposite is the home of their two elder sons and their wives. And the south house has been taken over by Wei. He's Jing's son, and he's living in the south house in preparation for his marriage.'

'He's the one I saw the other night? Married? He looks far too young.'

'He's twenty, but he's madly in love with Suyin, the girl who sang in the restaurant, and she seems to feel she can put up with him. Apart from him there are several other children, ranging from five to twelve. They're wonderful kids. Villains, mind you.'

'As the best youngsters always are.'

'Right,' he said, gratified.

'But how many people am I meeting?' she asked, beginning to be nervous.

'About eighteen.'

'Wow! I'm getting scared.'

'Not you. You're a dragon lady, remember? Brave, adventurous, ready for anything.'

'Thank you. But that big a family still makes me a bit nervous.'

'Eighteen isn't so many. There are at least another dozen in other parts of the country, and probably plenty more I have yet to meet.'

'Is that where you're going? You said something about travelling soon.'

'Something like that. Let's talk later. I must warn you that you're about to walk into the middle of a feud. Uncle Jing is furious with Uncle Hai because Hai's wife Biyu is cooking you dumplings. Jing thinks the privilege of cooking for you should have been his. He's a fishmonger, and also a wedding planner.'

'I've heard of that before,' Olivia said, much struck. 'It's because the words for fish and prosperity are so alike that fish gets served at weddings as a way of wishing the couple good luck. So fishmongers often plan weddings as well.'

'That's right. Hai does very well as an arranger of weddings, where of course he sells tons of his own fish. The trouble is he thinks he's entitled to arrange everything for everyone, and he's very put out about the dumplings.'

His solemn tone made Olivia burst out laughing.

'I promise to be tactful,' she said.

'Have I told you you're looking beautiful tonight?'

'Not a word.'

'Well, I'm being careful. If I said that deep blue does wonderful things for your eyes you'd find me very boring.'

'I might,' she said in a pensive voice. 'Or I might decide to forgive you.'

'Thank you, ma'am, but I feel sure you'd censure me for insulting you with that old-fashioned romantic talk. Heavens, this is the twenty-first century! Women don't fall for that kind of clap-trap any more.'

'Well, I wouldn't actually say any of that out loud,' she said, laughing.

'But you might think it silently, and that would be much worse. I'm wary of your unspoken thoughts.'

'But if they're unspoken you can't possibly know what they are,' she pointed out.

'You're wrong. I'm starting to understand the way you think.'

'That's an alarming prospect!' she observed.

'For which of us, I wonder?'

'For me,' she said without hesitation.

'Are you more alarmed at the thought of my getting it right, or getting it wrong?'

She considered this seriously. 'Right, I think. I don't mind you getting it wrong. I can always tread on your toes.'

'Good thinking.'

'But what woman wants to be understood too well by a man?' she mused.

'Most women complain that men don't understand them.'

'Then they're being foolish,' she said with a little smile. 'They should bless their luck.'

They both laughed and the moment passed, but she was left with the sense that beneath the banter they had really been talking about something else entirely. It was a feeling that often assailed her in Lang's company.

They continued the journey in companionable silence, until at last he said, 'Before we get there I'd better warn you of just how enthusiastically Wei has prepared them for you. I've explained that we barely know each other, and he mustn't run ahead, but he— Well…'

'Didn't take any notice?' Olivia finished sympathetically.

'And how!'

'All right, I'm prepared.'

'Grandfather Tao and Grandmother Shu have learned a few words in English, in your honour. The rest of the family speaks English, but those two are so old that they've lived a different kind of life. They've been practising all day to offer you this courtesy.'

'How kind.' She was touched. 'I know I'm going to love your family.'

At last she found herself in streets that she recognised.

'Weren't we here the other night?'

'Yes, that restaurant is just around the corner. Just a couple more streets, and here we are. Home.'

The car drew up before the north house of the *siheyuan*, and Olivia drew an astonished breath as she saw what looked like the entire family gathered to meet her. They spilled out of the doorway into the street.

In the centre stood an old man and woman: Grandfather Tao and Grandmother Shu. On either side of them were two middle-aged men—the uncles, their wives and children. Everyone was watching the car's arrival with delight, and two of the younger children dashed forward to open the door and provide Olivia with a guard of honour.

'My goodness!' she exclaimed.

Lang took her hand. 'Don't worry,' he whispered. 'I'm here, Dragon Lady.'

He slipped his arm protectively around her as they neared the family and it divided into two groups, with the oldest, Grandfather Tao and Grandmother Shu, at the centre. He took her to them first.

'Our family is honoured to meet you,' Tao said, speaking in careful, perfect English, and his wife inclined her head, smiling in agreement.

'It is I who am honoured,' Olivia said.

Tao repeated his compliment. The words and manner were formal but his and Shu's expressions were warm, and their eyes followed her when she moved on.

Strictly speaking they were the host and hostess, but because of their age and frailty they performed only the most formal duties, delegating anything more energetic to the younger ones.

Although brothers, Hai and Jing were totally unalike. Jing was a great, good-natured bull of a man, tall, broad and muscular. Beside him Hai was like a mountain goat next to a gorilla, small, thin and sprightly, with a wispy beard and bright eyes.

As the elder, Hai was introduced first, then his brother, then their wives—starting with Biyu, wife of Hai, and Luli, wife of Jing. They too greeted her in English, which she appreciated, but Lang immediately said in Chinese, 'No, she speaks our language. I told you.'

They repeated their greetings in Mandarin and

she responded accordingly, which made them
smile with pleasure.

'Mrs Lang—' Olivia started to say, but there
was a burst of laughter from several Mrs Langs.

'You can't say that,' Hai's wife declared
merrily. 'There are so many of us. Please, call me
Biyu.' She introduced the others as Ting, Huan,
Dongmei, and Nuo.

There seemed to be at least a dozen grown-up
youngsters, young men who studied Lang's lady
with politely concealed admiration, and young
girls who considered her with more open interest.
The fact that Olivia had the figure to wear a
cheongsam was particularly appreciated among
her contemporaries.

It was a warm evening, and the first part was to
be spent in the courtyard flanked by the four houses.
Here tables had been laid out with a variety of small
edibles, a foretaste of the banquet to come. Before
anything was served, Biyu led her into the south
house where Lang lived with Wei, and opened the
door to a bedroom with its own bathroom.

'Should you wish to retire for a few moments
alone,' she said, 'you will find this place useful.'
She saw Olivia glance around at the room's functional, masculine appearance, and said, 'When
Lang stays with us, this is his room, but this evening it is yours.'

'Thank you. I'll just refresh my face.'

'I'll be outside.'

Left alone, Olivia was able to indulge her frank curiosity, although she learned little. There were several books, some medical, some about China, but nothing very personal. Lang had revealed as little as possible about himself.

She went out to find that he had joined Biyu, and together they escorted her to where everyone was waiting. Now it was the turn of the children to crowd round. Just as she'd predicted, they called Lang 'Uncle Mitch', and even his adult relatives referred to him as Mitchell.

Glancing up, she caught his eye and he nodded, reminding her of the moment on the first evening when she'd anticipated this.

'The dragon lady always understands before anyone else,' he said lightly.

The children demanded to know what he meant by 'dragon lady'. He explained that she'd been born in the year of the dragon, and they regarded her with awe. Her stock had definitely gone up.

The children were frankly curious, competing to serve her and to ask questions about England. She answered them as fully as she could, they countered with more questions and the result was one of the most satisfying half-hours that she had ever spent. By the time they went inside to eat, the atmosphere was relaxed.

Olivia soon understood what Lang had meant about a feud. From the start the food was laid out like a banquet being displayed to her, dumplings in the place of honour, and a multitude of fish dishes which Hai kept trying to nudge to the fore, only to be beaten back by fierce looks from Biyu. To please them both, Olivia ate everything on offer and was rewarded with warm looks of pleasure.

Then she had a stroke of luck. Enquiring politely about Tao's life, she learned that he had once been a farmer. It happened that one of her mother's passing fancies had owned a small pig-farm where they had spent the summer. The relationship hadn't lasted, her mother having been unable to endure the quiet country life, but the fourteen-year-old Olivia had loved it. Now she summoned memories of that happy time, and she and Tao were soon in animated discussion. Pigs had provided Tao with a good living, and Olivia had enjoyed feeding time.

'There was a huge sow,' she recalled. 'She had a litter of fifteen, but only fourteen teats, and terrible fights would break out between the piglets over the last teat. I used to take a feeding bottle to make sure I could give something to the one who missed out. He'd just drink his fill and then go back to the fight.'

Tao roared with laughter and countered with the tale of a vast pig he'd once owned, who'd fathered larger litters than any other pig, and whose services had been much in demand among his neighbours. Everyone else round the table watched them with delight, and Olivia knew she'd scored a success by impressing the head of the family.

When the meal was over, Biyu showed her around the other houses. She was eager to know about her first meeting with Lang, and laughed at the story of the mischievous child.

'We are so proud of Mitchell,' Biyu said. 'He works very hard, and he's a big man at the hospital.'

'What does he actually do there?' Olivia asked. 'He was taking a clinic when we met, but apparently he was just filling in because they were short-staffed. I understand that his real job is something quite different.'

'That's true. He's a consultant.'

'A consultant?' Olivia echoed, amazed. 'He's young for that.'

'Oh, yes, he's only a *junior* consultant,' Biyu amended hastily. 'He keeps insisting on that. He gets cross if I make him sound too important—but I say he's going to be very, very important, because they know he's the best they have. There's a big job coming soon.'

She gave a knowing wink.

'You think he'll get it?'

'He will if there's any justice,' Biyu said firmly. 'But he's superstitious. He thinks if he gets too confident then some great power above will punish him by taking the job away from him.'

'Superstitious,' Olivia mused. 'You wouldn't think it.'

'Oh, he acts as if nothing could worry him,' Biyu confided. 'But don't you be fooled.'

It struck Olivia that this was shrewd advice. Lang's air of cool confidence had cracks, some of which he'd allowed her to see. The rest he seemed to be keeping to himself while their mutual trust grew.

'You're very proud of him, aren't you?' she said.

'Oh, yes. It was a great day for us when he came to China. We already knew a lot about him because Meihui had kept in touch, sending us news, and to see him was wonderful. The best thing of all was that he wanted to come, and then he wanted to stay. Some men from his country would have ignored their Chinese heritage, but he chose to find it and live with it, because it's important to him.'

'He's going away soon, isn't he, to do some exploring?'

'Actually, I thought he'd be gone by now. He spoke as though— Well, anyway, I'm glad he decided to wait a little longer, or we might not have met you.'

She tensed suddenly as Lang's voice reached them from outside.

'We're here,' she called back, showing Olivia out into the courtyard where he was waiting.

'Grandfather wants to bring out the family photographs,' he said. 'He's got hundreds of them, all ready to show Olivia.'

'And I'm longing to see them,' she said.

The largest room in the north house had been laid out in preparation, with a table in the centre covered in photographs. To Olivia's amazement the pictures stretched back sixty years to when Meihui had been a beautiful young girl. She must have been about sixteen in the first one, sitting in the curve of Tao's arm. His face as he looked down on his little sister bore an expression of great pride, and Olivia thought she could still see it there now as he regarded her picture. He was almost in tears over the little sister who had meant the world to him, and who he'd last seen when she was eighteen, departing for ever with the man she loved.

'And that's him?' Olivia asked as an Englishman appeared in the pictures.

'That's John Mitchell, my grandfather,' Lang agreed.

He seemed about twenty-three, not particularly handsome but with a broad, hearty face and a smile that beamed with good nature. Meihui's eyes, as she gazed at him, were alight with joy.

Then there were photographs that she had sent from England: herself and John Mitchell, proudly holding their new-born son, Lang's father. Then the child growing up, standing between his parents, until his father vanished because death had taken him far too soon. After that it was just Meihui and her son, until he married, and soon his own son appeared, a toddler in his father's arms.

'Let's leave them,' Lang groaned.

'But you were a delightful child!' Olivia protested.

He gave a grimace of pure masculine embarrassment, and she hastily controlled her mirth.

It was true that he seemed to have been a pleasant youngster, but even then his face held a sense of resolution beyond his years, already heralding the man he would become.

There were some pictures with his parents, then with his mother after his father's death, but mostly they showed the young Lang with Meihui. Then he appeared with his new family after his mother's remarriage. Looking at them, Olivia understood what he'd meant about not having been at ease. His step-father looked as though he had much good nature, but no subtlety, and his offspring were the same. Standing in their midst, the young Lang smiled with the courteous determination of a misfit.

He grew older, graduated from school and passed his medical exams. One picture especially caught Olivia's attention—it showed him sitting down while Meihui stood behind him, her hands on his shoulders, her face beaming with pride. At that moment she had been the happiest woman in the world. Instead of looking at the camera, Lang was glancing up, connecting with her.

'No wonder your family recognised you at the airport,' she murmured, drawing him slightly aside. 'Thanks to Meihui, they'd been with you every step of the way while you were growing up.'

'Yes, they said much the same. It made me feel very much at home.'

He spoke just loud enough for Biyu to hear, making her glance up and smile. He smiled back, yet strangely Olivia sensed a hint of tension in him, the last thing she'd expected. Now she thought about it, she felt there was a watchfulness about him tonight that wasn't usually there.

She wondered if she was the cause of his concern, lest she make a bad impression, but his manner towards her was full of pride. What was troubling him, then? she wondered.

As they left the room, Biyu announced, 'Now I'm going to show you our special place, devoted to Jaio and Renshu. I know Lang has told you about them.'

'Yes, it must be wonderful having such a great family tradition, going back so far.'

'It is. We have mementoes of them which normally we keep locked away for safety, but in your honour we have brought them out.' She gave a teasing smile. 'Lang tells us that you may need a little convincing.'

'Oh, did he? Just wait until I see him.'

'You mean, it isn't true?' Biyu asked.

'Of course— Well, I think it's a lovely story.'

'But perhaps a little unreal?' Biyu sighed. 'The world is so prosaic these days. People no longer believe in a love so great that it conquers everything. But few families have been as fortunate as we. We keep our mementoes because they are our treasures, not in the worldly way, but treasures of the heart. Come, let me show you our temple.'

Crossing the courtyard, she entered the south house that would soon belong to Wei and his bride.

'This is where we keep our temple,' she said, opening the door to a room at the back. 'Wei and his wife-to-be have promised to respect it.'

It was a small room. In the centre was a table on which some papers were laid out, and a piece of jade.

'These are our mementoes of them,' Wei said.

'Those papers,' Olivia said. 'They are actually the ones that—?'

'The very ones that were discovered after their deaths.'

'Two-thousand years ago,' Olivia murmured.

She tried to keep a touch of scepticism out of her voice. She liked Biyu, and didn't wish to seem impolite, but surely nothing could be certain at such a distance of time?

'Yes, two-thousand years,' Biyu said. 'We've had collectors offering us a lot of money for them, saying that they are valuable historical relics. They cannot understand why we will not sell. They say the money would make us rich.'

'But these are beyond price,' Olivia said.

Biyu nodded, pleased at her understanding.

'Their value is not in money,' she agreed.

'What do the papers say?' Olivia asked. 'Normally I can read Chinese but these are so faded.'

'They say "We have shared the love that was our destiny. Whether long or short, our life together has been triumphant. They say that love is the shield that protects us from harm, and we know it to be true. Nothing matters but that".'

'Nothing matters but that,' Olivia murmured.

How would it feel to know a love so all-embracing that it extinguished everything else in the world? She tried to remember her feelings for Andy, and realised that she couldn't recall his face. Now there was another face on the edge of her consciousness waiting to be allowed in, but only when she was ready.

A man with the gift of endless patience could be comforting, fascinating, perhaps even alarming. She hadn't yet decided.

'I will never forget the day we showed these to Lang,' her hostess said. 'He had heard of them from Meihui, but the reality was very powerful to him. He held them in his hands and kept saying, "It is really true".'

'I love the way you all feel so close to Lang,' Olivia said. 'You don't treat him differently at all.'

'But should we? Oh, you mean because he's a little bit English?'

'Three-quarters English,' Olivia said, laughing.

Biyu shrugged as if to say 'what is three quarters?'.

'That is just on the surface,' she said. 'In here—' she tapped her heart '—he is one of us.'

Lang came in at that moment and Olivia wondered if he'd heard these last words. If he had they must surely have pleased him, but it was hard to tell.

'There's a little more,' he said, indicating a side table where there were two wooden boxes and two large photographs which Olivia recognised as Meihui and John Mitchell.

'The boxes are their ashes,' Biyu confided, looking at Lang. 'He brought them.'

'Meihui kept John's ashes,' Lang said. 'And when she died I promised her that I would bring them both here.'

'We had a special ceremony in which we welcomed them both home and said that we would always keep them together,' Biyu said. 'And we laid them in this temple, so that Renshu and Jaio could always watch over them.'

She spoke with such simple fervour that Olivia's heart was touched. It didn't matter, she realised, whether every detail of the legend was exactly true. The family had taken it as their faith, and perhaps a trust in the enduring power of love was the best faith anyone could choose.

Silently, Biyu drew her attention to a hanging on the wall. It was a large sheet of parchment, and on it were written the words Jaio had spoken: *love is the shield that protects us from harm*.

In the end their love hadn't protected them from those who'd sought them out, but now Olivia knew that this wasn't the harm Jaio had meant. To live a lonely, useless life, separated from the one who could give it meaning—that was a suffering neither she nor Renshu had ever known. And, if there had been a price, they did not complain.

She began to understand a little more of the family's pride in Lang, the man who through his grandmother embodied the legend in the present day.

He was looking away at that moment so that she was able to observe him unseen. And it seemed to her that the mysterious 'something' in his face was now more evident than ever.

CHAPTER SIX

As it grew dark the lanterns came on in the court-yard and everyone gathered to hear Suyin sing. After a while Olivia slipped away and went to Lang's room in the south house, glad of a moment alone to mull over what she'd learned tonight. She was beginning to understand Lang a little better—he was a man who hung back behind a quiet, even conventional mask, but who behind that mask was a dozen other men. Some of those men were fascinating, and some she should perhaps be wary of.

After giving her hair a quick brush, she left the room and found him waiting in the hall outside. She faced him with an air of indignation that was not entirely assumed.

'I've got a bone to pick with you,' she said.

'Are you mad at me? I've offended you?'

'Don't you give me that deferential stuff. I see right through it. You can't open your mouth without fooling me about something.'

'What have I done now?'

'I asked you about your job and you gave me the impression that you were little more than the hospital porter. Now I find out you're an important man.'

'I deny it,' he said at once.

'A consultant.'

'*Junior* consultant. It's just a title that's supposed to make me feel pleased with myself. The real big man is the senior consultant.'

'Oh, really? And when is the big man going to retire and let you step into his shoes?'

'That's a long story. We should be getting back before they come looking for us.'

He was still smiling, but she had a feeling that she'd touched a nerve. The hospital was one of the biggest and most important in Beijing. If he was seriously hoping for a major promotion after only three years, then he was more ambitious than he wanted anyone to know.

'They've already come to seek us out. There they are,' Lang said, indicating outside where Biyu could be seen watching, accompanied by Wei, Suyin and an assortment of children. 'From where they're standing, you can see in through the window, and they're waiting to see if we fulfil expectations.'

This was so plainly true that she chuckled.

Some people would have found the blatant curiosity intrusive and dismaying, but Olivia—child of a fractured family where there had been much hysterical emoting but little genuine kindness— felt only the warmth of a large family welcoming her, similar to what Lang himself had felt, she guessed.

'Then you'd better put your arm around my shoulders,' she said.

'Like that?' His hand rested lightly on her shoulder.

'I think you might manage to be a little more convincing,' she reproved him. 'We're supposed to be giving them what they want, and I doubt if they can even see anything from there.'

'You're right,' he agreed. 'It has to look real.'

Tightening his arm, he drew her closer to him. Slowly he lowered his head until his lips were just brushing hers.

'Is this real enough?' he murmured.

'I think—I think we might try a little harder.'

That was all the encouragement he needed. Next moment his mouth was over hers forcefully. There was no hesitancy now, but a full-scale declaration of intent; his lips moved urgently, asking a question but too impatient to await the answer.

Olivia responded with an overwhelming sense of relief. She had wanted this, and it was only now that she knew how badly. Since their first meeting she'd been fighting him on one level, responding on another. Now she was no longer torn two ways and could yield to the delight that flowed through her with dizzying speed.

She'd demanded that he be more convincing, and he was following her wishes to the letter. But then he lifted his head for a moment and she saw the truth in his eyes. The one brief touch of lips that they'd shared the day before had given barely a hint of what awaited them, and now he was as stunned as she by the reality.

'Olivia…'

'Don't talk,' she said huskily, pulling his head down.

Then there was only a silence more eloquent than words. She'd studied his mouth, not even realising she was doing so, wondering how its shape would feel against her own. Her imaginings had fallen far short of this overwhelming awareness of leashed power combined with subtlety.

He released her mouth and dropped his head so that his breath warmed her neck softly. He was trembling.

She wanted to say something, but there was nothing to say. No words would describe the feelings that pervaded her, feelings that she wanted to go on for ever. Tenderly she stroked his head, turning slightly so that they could renew the kiss. She wanted that so badly.

But one of the children outside gave an excited squeal and was hastily shushed. The noise seemed to come from a distance, yet it shattered the spell ruthlessly. Stranded back on earth again, they regarded each other in bewilderment.

'I think,' Lang said unsteadily, 'I think we'd better—'

'Yes, I guess we should,' she replied, not having the least idea what she was talking about.

They walked out, bracing themselves for an ironic cheer, but the others had melted tactfully away. They'd seen all they needed to.

When it was time to leave, everyone embraced her warmly. Tao and Shu presented her with a glass pig, insisting that she must come again soon, and everyone stood outside to wave them off.

Lang drove in silence. Olivia wondered if he would speak about what had happened, but she was neither surprised nor disappointed when he didn't. It wasn't to be spoken of.

'Let's stop for a while before we go home,' he said at last. 'There's a little place just down here.'

It turned out to be a teahouse constructed on old-fashioned lines, several connected buildings with roofs that curved dramatically up at the corners. Red lanterns hung inside, and stretched out to a small garden. They went to an outside table where their tea was served in elegant porcelain cups.

Lang wished he knew what to say. He'd come here hoping for time to think after having been disconcerted all evening. He'd wanted Olivia to make a good impression on his family, but she'd done more than that. She'd been a knockout. He smiled, remembering how brilliantly she'd swapped pig memories with Grandfather Tao, and how his female relatives had been won over by her fashion sense.

He'd been astonished, but he should not have been. In the brief time he'd known her she'd taken him by surprise more often than he could count. It was alarming—it turned the world on its head in a way that constantly caught him off-guard—but it was also part of her charm.

As an attractive man he was used to having women put themselves out to get his attention. He wasn't conceited about it, he just didn't know any different. Now he was relishing an experience that nothing had prepared him for.

To find himself powerfully attracted to a woman who was fighting her own attraction to him, to have to persuade her and tease her into a sense of security so that he could convince her of the value of romantic love, intrigued him and made him wonder just where this road was leading.

Wherever it led, he knew that he was happy to go there, and that the time of decision had come. He must act now or lose what might be the most precious gift of his life.

The courtyard of the teahouse was enclosed on three sides. On the fourth there was a small pond where ducks quacked for titbits, and a bridge where they could linger after drinking their tea.

'Oh, this is so nice.' Olivia sighed, enjoying deep breaths of the sweet air and tossing a crumb into the water. She'd taken a small cake from the table for this purpose, but had eaten none of it herself.

'Are you sure you don't want anything else?' Lang asked.

She laughed. 'No, the tea was delicious and I've had enough food to last me for a month. It was wonderful food. I'm not complaining.'

'I am,' he said frankly. 'It felt like being fattened for the slaughter. They were in competition to see which one of us they could make collapse first.'

'But they're so nice,' Olivia said. 'It was all so warm and friendly, just like a family should be.'

'I'm glad you felt that. I love them dearly, but I was afraid you might find them a little overpowering.'

'I did.' She laughed. 'But I don't mind being overpowered with kindness. Not one bit.'

She tossed another crumb into the water and

watched the quacking squabble. At last she said, 'Biyu mentioned something strange—apparently they'd expected you to be gone before now.'

He hesitated a brief moment before admitting, 'I stayed because of you. I didn't mean to. I've been packed and ready to go for several days, but I couldn't make myself leave, or even make up my mind to come and talk to you.'

She nodded. The discovery that his confusion matched her own seemed to draw them closer.

'When do you leave for the Yangzte cruise?' he asked.

'I join the boat at Chongqing in a couple of days.'

'I've been planning to go to Xi'an,' he said thoughtfully.

'To see the mausoleum that Jaio escaped?'

'In a way. It hasn't been excavated yet, so I can't go inside, but I can see the terracotta warriors nearby. They were based on the Emperor's army.'

'So one of them might be Renshu,' she supplied. 'It sounds a great trip, but if you've been in China for three years I can't understand why you haven't been there before.'

'I have. It was one of the first places I went. But since I've lived here for a while I see things with different eyes. Then I was still a stranger. Now I feel part of this country, and I want to retrace my steps and try to understand things better.' Suddenly he grasped her hand and said, 'Olivia?'

'Yes?'

He took a deep breath and spoke with the eagerness of a man who'd finally seen the way clear.

'Come with me. Don't say no. Ah, say you'll come.'

It was only when she heard Lang beg her that Olivia fully understood how desolate she would have been if he'd left without a backward glance at her.

Don't get flustered, said the voice within. You're a woman of the twenty-first century. Stay cool.

'You mean, to see the warriors?' she asked with a fair display of casualness.

'I want to find out if I can make you see them as I do. Or maybe you'll show me something I've missed.' He added reflectively, 'You have a way of doing that.'

'It's quite unconscious.'

'I know. That's why it's so alarming. It springs out at me suddenly, and I have no chance to guard against it.'

'Do you want to guard against it?'

'Sometimes.'

She waited, sensing that he had more to say, and at last he went on. 'Sometimes you take fright and want to flee back to your old, safe life where things follow a pattern and nothing is too unpredictable. But then you realise that that's a kind of death; the safety is an illusion, and there's nothing to do but take the next step—whatever it brings. And sometimes—' he made a rueful face '—you can't decide between the two.'

'I know,' she murmured, awed by his insight.

'I'm a coward,' he said. Looking up, he added, 'But maybe I'm not the only one.'

She nodded.

'Now and then,' she said slowly, 'what passes for common sense is only cowardice in disguise.'

'Does that mean you'll come with me or not?' he asked urgently. 'We could leave for Xi'an tomorrow, and go on to Chongqing afterwards, if you wouldn't mind my joining you on the cruise. And after that, well, we go wherever we fancy and do whatever we fancy.'

'Whatever we fancy,' Olivia murmured longingly. 'I wonder…'

He drew her down the far side of the bridge and under the trees. There in the shadows he could take her into his arms and remind her silently of the things that united them. She came willingly, letting her own lips speak of feelings for which there were as yet no words.

She ought to refuse; she knew that. Step by seemingly innocent step he was enticing her along a path she'd sworn never to tread again, a path on which the delight in one man's presence would silence all warnings until her life spun into turmoil. How virtuous it would be to be strong. How sensible. How justified! How impossible!

With every caress his mouth begged her to trust him with her heart and follow him to an unknown destination. Except that it wasn't really unknown. It was the place where he wanted to be with her, and no questions were needed.

He kissed her again and again, breathing hard as his urgency and need threatened to overcome his control.

'We'll have the whole summer together,' he managed to say. 'That is, if the idea pleases you.'

'It pleases me,' she said softly.

A violent tremor went through him. He was resting his forehead against her, his eyes closed while he fought to subdue himself. She held him with passionate tenderness, waiting, wondering what was happening behind his eyelids, and half-convinced that she knew.

At last he drew away and spoke in a shaking voice.

'Then let us make the arrangements quickly.'

He led her back to the table, took out his phone, and in a few brief calls changed her flights, booked her into his hotel in Xi'an, and just managed to grasp the last available place on the Yangtze cruise.

Then a silence fell. Both suddenly felt embarrassed, as though the emotion that had brought them thus far had abandoned them, leaving them stranded in alien territory where nothing looked the same.

'Perhaps we should go home and start getting ready,' he said awkwardly.

'Yes—packing.'

Lang had recovered his composure and gave her a mischievous look. 'Don't forget to include that dress you're wearing.'

'Oh, do you like it? I wasn't sure it suited me.'

'Stop fishing. You know exactly what it does for you. And if you didn't know at the start,' he added, 'you do now.'

'Yes,' she said, feeling her heart beat faster. 'I know now.'

'Let's go.'

At her door he said, 'I'll be here for you at midday tomorrow.'

He gave her a brief peck on the cheek and drove away.

She began her packing in a dissatisfied frame of mind and grew more dissatisfied as she lay wakeful overnight. Her mood was nothing to do with Lang and everything to do with the fact that her wardrobe was inadequate. The only really glamorous item she possessed was the *cheong-sam*, and something had to be done—fast.

When buying the *cheongsam* she'd lingered over several other items, wanting them but too prudent to spend the money.

But now she was going away with Lang, and to blazes with prudence.

He wouldn't arrive until noon. The shop was three streets away, and a quick dash there and back in a taxi would enable her to collect what she needed and return before him. She took her suit-cases down to the front door, and spoke to the tenant of the downstairs apartment.

'If a man calls for me, will you tell him I'll be back in ten minutes? Thanks.'

She called a taxi and waited for it outside, waving cheerfully at a little girl from one of the other apartments who was playing nearby. The taxi was prompt and she took off, managing to be back barely five minutes after midday. With luck, she thought, Lang wouldn't be there yet—but it wasn't really a surprise to find him ahead of her. What did surprise her was the volcanic look on his face.

'Where the devil have you been?' he demanded explosively.

'Hey, cut it out!' she told him. 'I'm a few minutes late. It's not the end of the world. I went to do a bit of last-minute shopping. I left you a message with the woman who lives downstairs. Didn't you see her?'

'The only person I've seen is a child who was playing here. She said you got into a taxi and went away *for ever*. That was her exact phrase.'

Olivia groaned. 'I know who you mean. She saw me get into the taxi but the rest is her imagination. I just went to buy something. I'm here now. Have you been waiting long?'

'Five minutes.'

She stared. 'Five minutes? That's nothing. No need to make a fuss.'

For answer he slammed his hand down hard on the bonnet of the taxi, causing the driver to object loudly. While they sorted it out, Olivia dashed inside to retrieve her suitcases.

She was stunned at what she'd just seen. Lang was the last man she would have suspected of such an outburst. Here was a troubling mystery, but her dismay faded as she emerged from the building and saw his face. It was no longer angry, but full of a suffering he was fighting to hide.

The driver, placated by a large tip, helped them load the bags, and then they were off.

In the taxi Olivia took Lang's hand and rallied him cheerfully. 'We're going to have a great time. Don't spoil it by being mad at me.'

'I'm not. I'm mad at myself for making a

mountain out of a molehill. After all, what's five minutes? That's the trouble with being a doctor, you get to be a stickler for time.'

He went on talking, turning it into a joke against himself. But Olivia knew it wasn't a joke really. It wasn't about five minutes; just what it was about was something she had yet to learn. In the meantime, she fell in with his mood, and they went to the airport in apparently good spirits.

The flight took two hours, and they reached the hotel in the evening.

'Is your room all right?' Lang asked as they went down to the restaurant.

'Yes, I'm going to sleep fine. Not that I plan to do much sleeping. I've still got a lot of reading to do about the Emperor.'

'I saw you buried in a book on the plane. Good grief, you've brought it down here with you.'

'He fascinates me. He took the throne of Qin when he was only thirteen, unified all the states into one country, standardised money, weights and measures, built canals and roads. But he only lived to be fifty, and he seems to have spent the last few years of his life trying to find a way to avoid death.'

'Yes, he dreaded the idea of dying,' Lang agreed. 'He sent court officials all over the world with orders to find a magic elixir. Most of them simply vanished because they didn't dare go back empty-handed. He tried to prolong his life by taking mercury, but that's probably what killed him so soon.'

'Which makes it all the more ironic that he had over half a million men building his tomb for years.'

'That was the convention. The pharaohs in Egypt used to do the same thing—start building their pyramids as soon as they ascended the throne.'

'And in the end all those poor, innocent women were trapped in there with him.' She sighed. 'What a pity we can't see inside.'

So far the tomb had not been excavated, although radar investigations had suggested many things of interest, including booby traps and rivers of mercury. Olivia knew that it would probably be several years before visitors could go into the tomb and see the place where Jaio would have died if Renshu hadn't rescued her.

In the meantime there was the other great sight to be seen, the terracotta warriors, buried nearly a mile away from the tomb and discovered thirty-five years earlier by farmers who'd happened to be digging in a field. The inspiration for these statues had been the men who protected the Emperor, of whom Renshu was one.

'I wonder how they met,' she mused now.

'Weren't the concubines kept strictly away from other men, except eunuchs?'

'Yes. The story is that Renshu was part of a group of soldiers who escorted her from the far city where she lived. Even so, he wasn't meant to see her face, but he did so by accident. The other story is that he was on duty in the palace one evening and caught a glimpse of her.'

'But could that be enough?' Olivia asked. 'They see each other for just a moment and everything follows from that?'

'Just a moment can be more than enough,' Lang mused. 'You never know when it's going to happen, or how hard it's going to hit you. You don't get to pick the person, either. She's just there in front of you, and it's her. She's the one.'

He gave a faint smile, aimed mainly at himself.

'Sometimes you might wish that she wasn't,' he said softly. 'But it's too late for that.'

'Oh, really? And why would you wish that she wasn't?'

'Lots of reasons. She might be really awkward. She might get you in such a state that you didn't know whether you were coming or going. You could go to bed at night thinking, "I don't need this. How can I get her out of my hair?" But the answer is always the same. You can't.

'And you come to realise that whichever one of

the deities decides these things isn't asking your opinion, just giving you orders…"There she is, she's the one. Get on with it".'

Olivia nodded. 'You say deity, but that voice can be more like a nagging aunt.'

'You too?' he asked slowly.

'Yes,' she said in a low voice. 'Me too. You try to explain to the aunt that she's got it all wrong—you weren't planning for anything like this guy—and all she says is, "Did I ask what you planned?"'

Lang laughed at her assumed hauteur. His eyes were warm as they rested on her.

'It's like being swept along by an avalanche,' Olivia continued. 'And sometimes you just want to go with it, but at other times you think—'

'Not yet?' Lang supplied helpfully.

'Yes. Just a little longer.'

She wished she could explain the sweet excitement he caused within her, and the caution she still had to overcome. But he came to her rescue, saying, 'I imagine Renshu felt the same when he fell in love with Jaio. He probably had a fine career in the army, and falling for the Emperor's concubine just spelled big trouble. He must have fought it, and maybe he kidded himself that he was succeeding, until her life was threatened, and then nothing else mattered. He knew he had to save her, and then he knew he had to be with her for ever— to love her, protect her, have children with her.'

His voice became reflective, as though he was just realising something.

'When he finally faced it, he was probably relieved. However hard the way ahead, he'd be at peace, because the big decision was made.'

'And yet he gave up so much,' Olivia mused. 'It was easier for her, she had nothing to lose, but he lost everything.'

'No, he gained everything,' Lang said quickly. 'Even though they didn't have very long together, she fulfilled him as nothing else ever could have done. And he knew that she would, or he'd never have gone to such lengths to make her his.'

'And yet think of how they must have lived,' Olivia said. 'On the run for the rest of their lives, never really able to relax because they were afraid of being caught.'

'I expect it was more than just being afraid,' Lang said. 'They probably knew for certain that one day they'd be caught and pay a heavy price. And, when it came, they were ready. The story is that when the soldiers found them Renshu tried to make Jaio escape while he held them off, but she went to stand beside him and they died together.'

'But what about their son?' Olivia asked. 'Shouldn't she have tried to live for his sake?'

'Her son had been rescued by the family. If she'd gone after him she would only have led the soldiers to him. Her choice was either to die in flight, or die at Renshu's side. To her there was really no choice at all. They knew what was coming. That's why they left those writings behind. They wanted to tell the world while there was still time.'

Olivia gazed at him in wonder.

'You speak as though you knew them, as though they were real people here with you this minute.'

'Sometimes that's just how it seems,' he confessed. He gave her a wry smile. 'No doubt you think that's ludicrously sentimental, you being such a practical person!'

'But you're a practical person too,' she pointed out. 'How could a doctor not be?'

'Yes, I'm a doctor, but that doesn't mean I only believe in things that can be proved in a test tube.'

'So a doctor can be as daft as anyone else?' she teased.

'Emphatically, *yes*. More so, in fact, because he knows what a false god scientific precision can be, and so he's wiser if he—'

He broke off abruptly and she guessed the reason. He was moving faster than her, so fast that perhaps he even alarmed himself.

But her alarm was fading. With every minute

that passed the conviction was growing in her that this was right. She didn't know what was lying in wait for them, but whatever it was she was ready, even eager, to find it.

CHAPTER SEVEN

AT LAST he said, 'If you've finished eating I think we should go upstairs. We need plenty of sleep.'

At her door he bid her goodnight with a brief kiss on the cheek before hurrying away, leaving her wishing he'd stay the same person for five minutes at a time.

She went to bed quickly and read some more of the book until finally she put it down and lay musing. After their talk that evening Renshu and Jaio seemed strangely real, and she had the feeling that tomorrow she was going to meet them. Face to face she would hear their story, about their life, about the love that was stronger than death. And perhaps she would understand a little more about the man whose existence had sprung from that love at a distance of two-thousand years.

Olivia turned out the light and went to the window. Opening it, she stood gazing out at the mountains that were just visible in the moonlight, and a thin line of silver where a river followed a curving course.

In the room beside hers, Lang's window was closed. She could see that his light was still on and, by leaning out, she could just see his shadow coming and going. She was about to call out to him when his light went off. She hurried back to bed and was soon asleep.

She awoke early, going to sit by the open window to breathe in the cool air and enjoy the view over the mountains now bathed in early-morning light. On impulse she took out her laptop and set up the connection with Norah. In England it would be mid-afternoon, not their usual time, but she might still make contact.

She was in luck. Almost at once Norah's face appeared on the screen. When the greetings were over, Olivia said, 'We're going to see the terra-cotta warriors.'

'I've heard of them. They're very famous.'

'Yes, but we have a special reason.'

Briefly she told the tale of Jaio and Renshu. As she'd expected, Norah was thrilled.

'So Lang is descended from a warrior and a concubine. What fun!'

'You're incorrigible,' Olivia said, laughing. Then something made her stop and peer more closely at the screen. 'Are you all right? You look a bit pale.'

'I've been out doing some shopping. It was nice, but very tiring.'

'Hmm. Come closer, so that I can see you better.'

'Stop fussing.'

'I just want to take a look at you.'

Grumbling, Norah moved until Olivia could see her better.

'There,' she said. 'Now stop making a fuss.'

Suddenly there came a knock on Olivia's bedroom door.

'Don't go away,' she said, drawing the edges of her light bathrobe together and heading for the door.

Lang was standing outside in a towel robe. He too pulled the edges together when he saw her.

'Are you all right?' he said. 'I heard you talking, and I wondered if anything's wrong.'

'I'm talking to Aunt Norah by video link. I promised her I'd stay in touch. Come and meet her.'

She showed him to the window chair and made him sit where the camera could focus on him.

'Here he is, Aunt Norah,' she said. 'This is Dr Lang Mitchell.'

'How do you do, Dr Mitchell?' Norah said formally.

'Please, call me Lang,' he said at once, giving the old woman his most charming smile. She responded in kind and they beamed at each other across five-thousand miles.

'And I'm Norah.'

'Norah, I can't tell you how I've looked forward to meeting you.'

'You knew about me?'

'Olivia talks about you all the time. At our very first meeting she told me that you said if she ever shut up she'd learn something.'

Olivia gaped, outraged, and Norah beamed.

'And I have to tell you,' Lang continued confidentially, 'that after knowing her only a short time I realise what a good judge of character you are.'

The two of them rocked with laughter while Olivia glared.

'You can leave any time you like,' she informed him coolly.

'Why would I want to leave? I've just made a new friend.'

He and Norah chatted on for a few minutes and Olivia regarded them, fascinated by the way they were instantly at ease with each other.

At last Lang rose, saying, 'It was delightful meeting you, and I hope we talk again soon.' To Olivia he said, 'I'll see you downstairs for breakfast.'

He left the room quickly. He needed to be alone to think.

The Chinese had a saying: 'it is easy to dodge a spear thrown from the front, but hard to avoid an arrow from behind'.

In Lang's mind the spear from the front had been the moment he'd arrived to collect Olivia and found that she'd already left, 'for ever'. For a few blinding, terrible minutes he'd been convinced that she'd changed her mind and left him, even fled the country, and that he would never see her again.

The moment when she'd appeared was burned into his consciousness with searing force. She hadn't left him. Everything was all right. Except that now he'd glimpsed a future that didn't contain her, and it appalled him.

He'd coped. He'd known already that his feelings for her were running out of control. It was only their extent that shocked him, and which had made him ultra-cautious in their talk over dinner the night before.

Harder to cope with were the arrows that struck unexpectedly. One had come out of nowhere earlier, giving him a bad fright.

He'd heard Olivia's voice as soon as he'd opened his window, and had smiled, thinking she was on the telephone. But the words, 'you look a bit pale' had told him this was no phone call. And while he'd been trying to take in the implications she'd added, 'Come closer, so that I can see you better.'

The idea of a video link hadn't occurred to him. He'd tried to stay cool, not to jump to the conclusion that she had a man in the room, but no power on earth could have stopped him knocking on her door to find out. Now he was feeling like the biggest fool of all time. Yet mixed in with embarrassment was delight that he'd been wrong. All was well.

The arrows would keep coming when he least expected them. He knew that now. But nothing could stop his mood rioting with joyful relief, and in the shower he gave vent to a yodelling melody. When he joined her downstairs, he was still lightheaded.

'I can see that Norah and I are going to be the best of friends,' he told her.

'Ganging up on me at every turn, I suppose.'

'Of course. That's half the fun. Did she say anything about me after I'd gone?'

'Not a word,' she declared loftily. 'We dismissed you from our minds.'

'As bad as that?' he said, nodding sympathetically.

'Worse. I couldn't get any sense out of her. She just wittered on endlessly about how handsome you are. Where she got that idea, I couldn't imagine.'

'The video quality is never very strong on those links.'

'Well, she likes you enormously.'

'Good. I like her too. Now, let's have a hearty breakfast and get revved up for the day.'

An hour later the coach called to collect them, plus several others from the hotel, and soon they were on the road to the warrior site.

'The thing I loved about it,' Lang said, 'was that they didn't build a separate museum and transport everything to it. They created the museum on top of the actual site of the dig where the figures were found.'

She saw what he meant as soon as they entered. The museum was divided into three huge pits, the first of which was the most astonishing. There in the ground were hundreds of soldiers standing in formation as though on duty. A gallery had been built all around so that the visitor could view them from every angle. This was exactly the place where they had been discovered and, as Lang had said, it made all the difference.

Not only men but horses stood there, patient unto eternity. After burial they had had only a short existence, for less than five years after the Emperor's death they had been attacked, many of them smashed and the site covered in earth. For over two-thousand years they had remained undiscovered, waiting for their time to come, silent and faithful in the darkness.

Now their day had dawned again. Some had been repaired and restored to beauty, although thousands still remained to be unearthed. Now they were world-famous, proud and honoured as they deserved to be.

Although Lang had been here before he too was awed as they walked around the long gallery.

'We've only seen a small part,' he said as he left. 'When we visit the rest you can study some of them close up. It's incredible how they were created so skilfully all that time ago—the fine details, the expressions.'

When Olivia saw the figures that were displayed in glass containers she had to admit that he was right. Not one detail had been skimped on the armour, and the figures stood or crouched in positions that were utterly natural. No wonder, she thought, that historians and art experts had gone wild about them.

But she wasn't viewing them as a professional. It was as men that they claimed her attention, and as men they were awesome, tall, muscular, with fine, thoughtful but determined faces.

'It's incredible how different they all are,' she mused. 'It would have been so easy to give them all the same face, but they didn't do it the easy way. How many of them are there?'

'Something like eight thousand when they've finished excavating,' Lang said. 'And I don't think they're all precisely individual. If you hunt through them you'll find the same face repeated now and then, but it's a long hunt.'

Their steps had brought them to a glass container with only one figure. He was down on one knee, but not in a servile way. His head was up, his back straight, his air alert, as though his whole attention was devoted to his duty.

'Whoever this was based on had a splendid career ahead of him,' she murmured. 'And he gave it all up.'

'You've decided that this was Renshu?' Lang asked, fondly amused.

'Definitely. He's by far the most handsome.'

Before finishing the tour, they went to the pavilion where there was a teahouse to refresh them.

'It's so real,' she said. 'I hadn't expected to find them so lifelike. You could almost talk to them and hear them talk back.'

'Yes, that's how I felt.'

'You know that story you told me—how he might have seen her when he was escorting her, or later in the palace—well, I've been thinking, and they could both be true. Renshu saw her face accidentally on the journey, and after that he knew he had to see her again, so he connived to get assigned to palace duty.'

'That's a very romantic suggestion,' Lang exclaimed. 'I'm shocked!'

'All right, I've weakened just a little. Now I've seen what a fine, upstanding man he must have been, I can understand why she fell in love with him.' Olivia laughed at the sight of Lang's expression. 'It's this place. Somehow the whole story suddenly seems so convincing. I can't wait to go back in.'

They spent the afternoon going over everything again, fascinated by the semi-excavated parts in pit one, where broken figures lay waiting to be reclaimed, and the places where they could study the work in progress. The day finished in the shop that sold souvenirs, and Olivia stocked up on books and pictures. Lang also was buying extensively.

'But you've got that book,' she said, pointing. 'I remember seeing it in your room.'

'It's not for me. It's a gift for my friend Norah.'

'That's lovely. She'll be so happy.'

Some of the other tourists were from their hotel and they all made a merry party, exchanging views on the way back. It was natural to join up again over the meal, and the evening passed without Lang and Olivia having a moment alone.

'When will you talk to Norah?' he asked later.

'Early tomorrow morning.'

'Make sure you call me so that I can talk to her.'

'Can I tell her you've bought her a present?'

'Don't you dare! I want to do that myself. Goodnight.'

'Goodnight.'

She contacted Norah early next morning and found her bright-eyed with anticipation.

'Where's Lang?' was her first question.

'Good morning, Olivia, how nice to speak to you,' Olivia said ironically. 'I gather I don't exist any more.'

'Let's say he rather casts you into the shade, my darling.'

'All right, I'll go and knock on his door.'

'Knock on his—? Do you mean he's in a different room?' Norah sounded outraged.

'Yes, we have separate rooms,' Olivia said through gritted teeth.

She hurried out, unwilling to pursue this subject further. After the way passion had flared between herself and Lang, it seemed inevitable that they would take the next step. But suddenly he seemed in no hurry, and hadn't so much as hinted that he might come to her at night.

Perhaps she had mistaken him and he wasn't as deeply involved as her, but both her mind and her heart rejected that thought as unbearable.

He returned with her and she witnessed again the immediate rapport between he and Norah as he showed her the gifts he'd chosen. For most of the conversation she stayed in the background.

'It's not like you to be lost for words,' he teased her when they had finished.

'I didn't want to spoil it for you two,' she teased back. 'You get on so well, I'm beginning to feel like a gooseberry.'

'Can you give me her address so that I can mail her present before we leave?'

She did so, and they parted, not to meet again until it was time to leave for the airport.

On the flight to Chongqing they fell into conversation with passengers on the other side of the aisle who were headed in the same direction, and before long several more joined in. Olivia brought out the catalogue showing *The Water Dragon*, the boat that would carry them down the Yangtze. It was a gleaming white cruise-liner, but smaller than an ocean vessel would be. It was ninety metres long and took one hundred and seventy passengers.

'That sounds just right,' somebody observed. 'Big enough to be comfortable, small enough to be friendly.'

'Yes, it's going to be nice,' Olivia agreed. She showed the catalogue to Lang. 'What do you think?'

'I think the restaurant looks good,' he said prosaically. 'I hope we get there soon. I'm hungry.'

When they landed a coach was waiting to take them the few miles to the river. Lang had fallen into conversation with an elderly lady who could only walk slowly, and he held back to assist her onto the coach, then sat beside her. Olivia settled down next to a young man who knew all about the river and talked non-stop.

At last the coach drew up at the top of a steep bank, at the bottom of which was the river, and *The Water Dragon*.

Olivia was first off and found herself swept forward by the crowd. Looking back, she saw that Lang was still helping the old lady. He signalled for her to go on without him, so she headed down the steps to the boat and joined other passengers milling around the chief steward. He gave them a smiling welcome, and declared that he was always at their service.

'Now I am going to show you to your cabins,' he said. 'You will find them all clean and comfortable, but if any of you should want something of a higher standard we have two upgrades available. Follow me, please.'

Out of the corner of her eye Olivia saw Lang, still with the old lady, giving her his kindest smile. She waved and turned away to follow the steward.

The cabins were, as he'd said, clean and comfortable, but on the small and spare side. Olivia sat on her narrow bed, looking around at her neat, efficient surroundings, and felt there was something lacking. Wasting no more time, she went looking for the steward.

'Can I see the upgrades, please?'

'I'm afraid only one is left.'

It was a luxurious suite with a living room, bathroom and a bedroom furnished with a huge bed that would have taken three. From the corridor outside came the sound of footsteps approaching. Someone else was going to inspect the place and she had one second to decide.

'I'll take it,' she told the steward.

He too had heard the footsteps and moved fast, whipping out a notepad and writing down her details. By the time the door opened, the transaction was complete.

'It's taken,' he sang out.

The newcomers, a man and a woman, groaned noisily and glared at Olivia.

'Can't we come to some arrangement?' the man demanded of Olivia. He was an oafish individual, built like an overweight walrus.

'Sorry, it's mine,' she told him.

'Aw, c'mon. You're on your own. What difference can it make to you?' he demanded belligerently. 'Here.' He flashed a wad of notes. 'Be reasonable.'

'Forget it,' she said firmly.

'Let me show you out,' the steward urged.

The man glared but departed. As he left she heard him say to his companion, 'Damned if I know what a woman alone needs with a place like this.'

It was a good argument, she thought wryly. Just what did she need with a huge double bed? She should stop being stubborn, admit that her own cabin was adequate and give up this delightful palace, possibly even take the money. That was what a sensible woman would do.

But suddenly she couldn't be sensible any more.

Lang, having been shown to his cabin, was also regarding it with dismay. When he'd suggested joining Olivia on the cruise, this functional little room wasn't what he'd had in mind. He considered taking an upgrade, but how was he to explain this to her? She would immediately suspect his motives, and the fact that her suspicions would be correct merely added to his problems.

But at last, annoyed with himself for dithering, he approached the steward, only to discover that he was too late. Both upgrade suites were taken.

'Surely there must be something?' he pleaded with the steward.

But this achieved nothing. He was left cursing himself for slowness, and generally despairing.

'You too?' said a man's voice behind him.

Lang turned and saw a large, belligerent-looking man scowling in frustration.

'They shouldn't give those upgrades to just anybody,' he snapped. 'We went for the top one—

nothing but the best for the missus and me—but it had already been taken by some silly woman who didn't need it.'

'Maybe she did need it,' Lang said.

'Nah, she was on her own, so why does she want to bother with a double bed? Hey, that's her over there in the green blouse— All right, all right.'

His wife was tugging his arm. He turned aside to squabble with her, leaving Lang in a daze.

Olivia was watching him across the distance, a slight smile on her face. He returned the smile, feeling delight grow and grow until it had stretched to every part of him. She began to move forward until she was standing in front of him, looking up, regarding him quizzically.

'I'm not sure what to say,' he told her.

'Don't tell me I've made you speechless?' she said, teasing and serious together.

'You do it often.'

The oaf had seen her and turned back to resume battle.

'Look, can't we talk…?' He fell silent, realising that neither of them was aware of him. They had eyes only for each other.

'Oh, well,' he mumbled at last. 'If it's like that.'

He let his wife drag him away.

Lang didn't speak, but he raised an enquiring

eyebrow as though the question was too awesome to be spoken aloud.

Olivia nodded.

'Yes,' she said softly. 'It's like that.'

From somewhere came the sound of footsteps, calls, engines coming to life, and there was a soft lurch as the boat began its journey.

'Let's go and watch,' he said.

She nodded, glad of the suggestion. The time was coming, but not quite yet.

Up on deck they watched as the boat glided gently into the middle of the river and started its journey downstream between the tall hills on either side. After a while they went to the rear where a blazing-red sun was beginning to set, sliding slowly down the sky.

To Olivia's eyes that setting sun seemed to be prophetic, marking the end of one thing and the beginning of another. Now she could no longer equivocate about her feelings for Lang, either to herself or to him. By seizing the chance of the upgrade, she'd given herself away, and she was filled with gladness.

No more pretence, no more hiding behind barriers that offered no real protection, no more denial that he had won her heart. She wanted to sing for joy.

'Isn't it wonderful?' she murmured.

He was standing behind her, his hands on her shoulders. 'Wonderful,' he said. 'And you know what would be even more wonderful?'

She leaned back. 'Tell me.'

He whispered softly in her ear. 'Supper.'

She jumped. 'What did you say?'

'I told you I was ravenous, and that was hours ago. They must be opening the restaurant about now.'

The joke was on her. She'd thought they were going to float away in misty romance, and all he cared for was his supper. But it wasn't really a delusion; the tenderness in Lang's face as he gazed down at her told her that.

'Let's go and eat before I fade to nothing,' he said.

'We'll do anything you want,' she vowed.

At that moment she would have promised him the earth.

The restaurant was a cheerful place with large tables where six people could crowd, calling cheerfully across at each other. But in one corner it was different. Olivia and Lang sat at a table small enough for only themselves, speaking little, sometimes looking out of the window at the banks gliding past in the gathering darkness.

He really was hungry, and ate as though his last meal had come. She left him to it, content to sit here in a haze of happiness thinking no further ahead than the night.

'I meant to get that upgrade too,' he said after a while. 'But it took me too long to pluck up the nerve.'

'Nerve? I always thought of you as a brave man.'

'About some things. Not everything.'

He poured her some wine before adding, 'You've always kept me wondering and I—don't cope with that very well. In fact, I'm beginning to think I don't cope with anything very well.'

She smiled at him tenderly. 'Do I look worried?'

'I don't think anything worries you, Dragon Lady. You're the most cool, calm and collected person I know.'

'It's an act,' she said softly. 'I'm surprised you were fooled.'

'Sometimes I was. Sometimes I hoped— Well, at first I was afraid to ask for the upgrade in case you felt I was rushing you.' He gave her a teasing smile. 'After all, we've only known each less than two weeks.'

Less than two weeks? Had it really only been over a week? Yet a lifetime.

'So maybe *I'm* rushing you?' she mused.

He didn't reply in words, but he shook his head.

As the diners came to the end of the meal the steward announced that they might like to gather in the bar where entertainment would be provided. The others hurried out leaving Lang and Olivia together. The steward approached, meaning to remind them cheerfully that they were missing the fun, but the words died unspoken as he became aware of the silence that united them.

Realising that they would never hear him, he moved quietly away. Neither of them knew he'd been there.

CHAPTER EIGHT

ALONE now, Lang and Olivia drifted up to the top deck. Darkness had fallen completely and the brilliant moon overhead showed the stark outline of the river.

Olivia had read about the Yangzte River; it was nearly four-thousand miles long and the third-longest river in the world. But nothing had prepared her for the reality.

Used to English waterways, where the sides were either gently sloping or completely flat, she was stunned by the height of these banks that loomed up almost like sheer cliffs on either side.

'They seem to go up for ever,' she said, leaning back against Lang. 'And they blot out everything. It's like a separate world.'

'Do you mind that?' he murmured against her hair. 'Do you want to go back to the other world where everything's in the right place?'

'And always the same place every time,' she

supplied. 'Until it isn't the right place any more. No, I don't want to go back to that.'

She sighed and raised her arms up to the moon that seemed to glide in a narrow river between the high cliffs.

'This is the world I want!' she cried. 'The one where I belong—but I never knew it.'

Lang dropped his head and she felt his lips against her neck. Yes, this was what a part of her had always known would happen. She'd thought herself safe in the tight little box she'd constructed to protect herself from feelings. And all the time the truth had been waiting for her, ready to pounce out of the darkness, catch her off-guard and fill her with joy.

Slowly she turned in his arms and looked up into his face, which she could just see in the ghostly light. Then he lowered his head and she forgot everything as his mouth touched hers, filling her with a delight that transcended anything she'd known before. All her life had been a preparation for this moment.

Their first proper kiss in his family's home had been thrilling, but it had contained a hint of performance for an audience. Their embrace in the teahouse garden had been sweet, but still they had lacked total privacy, and it hadn't been quite perfect.

Now they were alone with the moon, the sky and the mountains, alone in the universe, and the truth that was flowering between them was for no other eyes.

His kiss was gentle, his lips moving softly over hers, awaiting her response, then growing more urgent as he sensed her eagerness. She answered him in kind, exploring to see how much she tempted him, then relaxing as the answer became gloriously plain.

He kissed her mouth for a long time before moving to her eyes, her cheeks, even her chin. He was smiling.

'What is it?' she whispered.

'You've got such a pretty chin. I've always thought so. I promised myself that one day I'd kiss it.'

She laughed softly and felt his lips move down her neck to the base of her throat. The sensation was so pleasurable that she gave a long sigh of satisfaction and wrapped her arms about him, drawing him as close as possible.

They held each other in silence for a long time, then he stepped back, took her by the hand and together they went below deck.

The door into the suite opened noiselessly, and Olivia locked it behind them without turning on the light. For now they needed only the moonlight that streamed in through the window just behind the bedhead.

This man wasn't like other men. Even in the bedroom he didn't rush things, but took her into his arms again, kissing her slowly, giving her time to be ready for the next step. When he deepened the kiss she was ready, opening up to him from deep inside, eager for what they would exchange.

Slowly he drew her down onto the bed. She felt his fingers moving on the buttons of her blouse until it fell open and he was helping her remove it. When her breasts were free, he touched them almost reverently before dropping his head to caress them with his lips.

Olivia sighed with satisfaction and laid her hand on his head, letting her fingers run gently through his hair, tightening them slightly as the pleasure mounted then arching against him, inviting him to explore her further. He did so, starting to pull at the rest of her clothes, but not fast enough for her. She undid her own buttons, then his, opening his shirt wide and running her hands over his chest.

She had to discern it by touch and everything she found delighted her—the smoothness, the slight swell of muscles, the faint awareness of his heart beating.

'Tell me what you're thinking,' he murmured.

'I want you,' she said simply.

'I've always wanted you—is this really happening?'

'Yes. We can have anything—everything.'

As though the words were a signal, he hurriedly removed the last of his clothes and she did the same. They had known each other such a little time, yet they were both moved by the thought that they had been kept apart too long. Later they might talk about this, try to analyse it, but now there was only the urgency of leaping barriers, closing the distance, becoming one.

She opened her arms and he fell into them like a man coming home, loving her body and celebrating it with his lips and his hands, teasing and inciting her into an ecstasy of anticipation. Her head was spinning, her flesh thrumming with desire until at last they were united in one powerful movement, and she was claiming him as urgently as he claimed her.

She wanted it to last for ever, and for a few glorious moments anything seemed possible, but then it ended suddenly in an explosion of light and force that consumed her then threw her back to earth, gasping, reaching out into the darkness, no longer sure where she was or what was happening.

'Olivia…' Lang's voice reached her from a thousand miles away.

'Where are you?' she cried.

'Open your eyes, my love. Look at me.'

She did so, and found his face close to her. Even

in the darkness she could sense his profound joy, feel the smile on his lips as he pressed them against her cheek.

She lay there, breathing hard, trying to come to terms with what had happened to her. It was a loving beyond anything that she'd known in her life before, something that possessed her completely, but only because she was willing to be possessed.

'Don't go away,' she whispered, tightening her arms about him.

'I'm always here, if you want me.'

'I want you,' she said passionately. 'I want you. Hold me.'

He did so, keeping her against him while they both grew calmer. She was suffused by a sense of well-being such as she had never known before, as though everything in the world was right. She was where she was always meant to be, in the arms of the man who had been made for her, as she had been made for him. Of that she had not the slightest doubt.

'Do you remember what you said?' he asked softly. 'That we could have everything?'

'Wasn't I right?'

He shook his head. 'No, I've just found out that it isn't possible. Because, when you think you have everything, you discover that there's something more and you'll never reach the end. There will always be something more in you for me to find. And I will always want to find it.'

She nodded slowly. 'And I'll always want you to.'

He moved back carefully, looking down, trying to read her face in the moonlight. She smiled, and something in that smile seemed to reassure him, for he relaxed.

'I wondered how it would be,' he murmured. 'I knew we belonged together from the first moment we met.'

She raised an eyebrow and surveyed him with a touch of mischief.

'Really? You were very sure of yourself.'

'No, I was never that. You scared me. I wanted you so much that I was haunted by the fear of not winning you. I thought maybe there was another man, and when I found that there wasn't I couldn't believe my luck. I waited for you outside the school and pretended I was there as a doctor.

'I tried to be sensible. You'd have laughed if you could have seen my mental contortions. I didn't call you for several days because I was trying not to be too obvious, but you must have seen right through me.'

'Not quite,' she said with a memory of herself growing frustrated because he hadn't phoned.

'I did it all wrong. I left it so long to call you

that the school term came to an end and I thought you might have gone.'

'So that's why you came and haunted the gate?'

'And I practically kidnapped you. Didn't you notice?'

'I can't really remember. I was too busy for distractions.'

He regarded her in dismay. 'Really?'

She just laughed. Let him wonder.

'I thought you might have left early,' he resumed, 'and I'd have lost you through my own carelessness. I nearly fainted with relief when I saw you coming out of the school. After that, I did everything to make sure of you—asking you home to dinner—'

'*Asking?*'

'Yes, I didn't give you much chance to refuse, did I?' He grinned. 'But how could I? You might really have refused, and I couldn't chance that.'

'Then you were quite right not to take any risks. And when you *asked* me to go to Xi'an, and joined me on this boat, you didn't take chances about that, either. I barely had time to catch my breath.'

'That was the idea. I thought I'd got it all sewn up. I was insufferably pleased with myself, so I suppose I was really asking for fate to sock me on the jaw.'

'This I have to hear. How did it do that?'

'I arrived to collect you and you'd gone, "for ever".'

'It was just an accident.'

'I didn't know that. I thought you'd had enough of me and decided to get out fast. You might have left the country and vanished into thin air. I didn't know how to contact you in England, and I couldn't ask the school until term started weeks later. I nearly went mad.'

'You could have texted my mobile phone.'

'Not if you'd turned it off and blocked my calls,' he said glumly. 'Which you'd do if you were running away from me.'

She stared at him, astonishment at his vulnerability mingling with happiness that she affected him so strongly.

'You've really got a vivid imagination, haven't you?' she said.

'You arrived just in time to stop me going crazy.'

Light dawned. 'Is that why you slammed your hand on the taxi?'

'I had to do something. It was that or a heart attack. I'm not usually violent, it's just—I don't know—it mattered. And until then I hadn't faced how *much* it mattered.

'But I could tell you didn't like me getting so worked up, so after that I backed off, played it cool, so as not to alarm you.'

'I thought you were having regrets,' she whispered.

He shook his head and said in a slow, deliberate voice, 'If there is one thing I will never regret, it is you. If I live to be a hundred I shall still say that this was the supreme moment of my life. If you leave me tomorrow, I'll still remember this as the greatest joy I ever knew. I say that with all my heart and soul. No, don't speak.'

He laid his hand quickly over her lips, silencing what she would have said.

'Don't say anything now,' he urged. 'I don't want you to be kind, or say what you think I want to hear. I'll wait gladly until your feelings prompt you to speak. Until then, silence is better.'

She could have said everything at that moment, gladdening his heart with a declaration to match his own. But instinct warned her that his reticence sprang from a deep need, and the kindest thing she could do for him was to respect that need.

So she merely enfolded him in her arms, drawing him close in an embrace that was comforting rather than passionate.

'It's all right,' she whispered. 'It's all right. I'm here.'

In a moment they were both asleep.

She awoke in the early hours to find him still

lying across her in the same position. Everything about him spoke of blissful contentment.

Then he opened his eyes, looking at her. The same contentment was there, like a man who'd come home. It became a joyous, conspiratorial smile, the meaning of which they both understood. They had a shared secret.

Light was creeping in through the curtains over the window behind the bed. She pulled herself up in bed and drew the curtains back a little, careful in case they were passing another boat. But the river was empty. There was nobody to see her nakedness, so she moved up further. He joined her and they sat together at the window, watching a soft, misty dawn come up on the Yangtze, drifting slowly past.

It was like a new day in which the shapes were ill-defined, changing from moment to moment, but always beautiful, leading them on to more beauty and happiness.

Could you really start a new life like this? she wondered. Or was it nothing but a vague dream, too perfect to be true? And did she really want to know the answer just yet?

She slid down into the bed again, stretching luxuriously, and he joined her, laughing. Then he saw something on the side table that made him stare.

'Hey, what's this? Ming Zhi?' He took the little panda in his hand. 'You brought her with you?'

'I like to have her near as a reminder not to get carried away,' Olivia said.

He raised eyebrows. 'What happened last night?'

'I gave her time off.'

He set Ming Zhi down again and lay back, wrapping Olivia in his arms.

'If she's still off-duty, perhaps I should make the most of it.'

He didn't wait for her to answer, but covered her mouth forcefully and proceeded to 'make the most of it' in a way that left her no chance to argue even if she'd wanted to.

It was a riotous loving, filled with the sense of discovery that two people know when they have answered the first question and are eager to learn the others. This was an exploration, with more sense of adventure than tenderness, and when it was finished they were both gasping.

'I need my breakfast,' Lang said in a faint voice. He was lying flat on his back, holding her hand. 'Then I think I'll come back to bed.'

'Nonsense!' she declared in a hearty voice that made him wince. 'When the boat makes its first stop we're going to get out and do some sensible sight-seeing.'

'Not me. I'm staying here.'

'All right. You stay and I'll go. It'll give me a chance to get to know that very tall young man who came aboard in the same group as us.'

'You're a cruel woman. Help me up.'

They became conventional tourists, joining the crowds to see the sights, but always chiefly aware of each other. They were the first back on board, declaring themselves exhausted and badly in need of a siesta. Then they vanished for the rest of the afternoon.

'What shall I wear tonight?' she mused as they were dressing for dinner.

She held up the figure-hugging *cheongsam* and, to her surprise, he shook his head.

'I thought you liked it.'

'I do,' he said. 'When we're alone. But if you think I want every other man in the place gawping at you…'

'Fine, I'll wear it.'

From this he could not budge her. The ensuing argument came close to being their first quarrel, but the knowledge that he was jealous was like heady wine, driving her a little crazy.

When she was dressed, he growled, 'Don't even look at anyone but me,' clamping his arm around her waist to make his point.

'I wasn't going to,' she assured him. 'Unless, of course, I get up onstage.'

'Why should you do that?'

'They're having a talent contest for the passengers. I thought I'd do a striptease.'

'Try that and I'll toss you over my shoulder and carry you off caveman-style.'

'Mmm, is that a promise?'

'Wait and see.'

The boat was equipped with a tiny nightclub, with a stage just big enough for modest entertainment. One by one people got up and sang out of tune, to the cheers of their friends.

'Hey!' A young man tapped Lang on the shoulder. 'There's a group of us going to sing a pop song. Want to join us?'

'Thank you, but no,' Lang said. 'I can't sing.'

'Neither can we, but it won't stop us. Aw, come on. Don't you know how to have a good time?'

'I am having a good time,' Lang said, polite but unmoved.

The young man became belligerent. He had a good-natured, if slightly oafish face, but had drunk rather too much.

'You don't look it to me. It's supposed to be a party. Come on.'

Lang made no reply but merely sat with an implacable smile on his face. At last the oaf gave

up and moved away, but not before one parting
shot to Olivia.

'I feel sorry for you, luv, know what I mean? A
wimp, that's what he is.'

Olivia could have laughed out loud at such a
total misreading of Lang. But she only looked the
man in the eye, smiled knowingly and shook her
head. He understood at once and backed off.

'More to him than meets the eye, eh?' he queried.

'Much, much more,' she said significantly.

'Ah, well, in that case…'

He took himself off.

Lang eyed her. 'Thank you, dragon lady, for
coming to my defence.'

'Don't give me that. You don't need me or
anyone defending you.'

'True, but it's nice to know that you don't
consider me a wimp. Our vulgar friend can think
what he likes.'

'Well, you know exactly what he's thinking.'

He grinned. 'Yes, thanks to you he believes I'm
a cross between Casanova and Romeo.'

'He's not the only one. Look.'

Their tormentor had joined his fellows on the
stage and was whispering to them urgently,
pointing in Lang's direction.

'Oh, no!' Lang groaned. 'What have you done?'

'Given you a really impressive reputation.' She chuckled. 'You should be grateful to me.'

'Grateful? Let's get out of here.'

He hastily set down his glass, grabbed her hand and drew her away with more vigour than chivalry. By now the entire audience seemed to be in the know, and they were pursued by whistles of envy and appreciation.

Lang almost dragged her down the corridor and into their suite, where he pulled her into his arms and kissed her fiercely, both laughing and complaining together.

'Olivia, you wretch! I'll never be able to show my face again.'

'Nonsense, you'll be a hero.' She chuckled, kissing him between words.

'Come here!'

He drew her firmly down on the bed and lay on top of her, pinning her down, his eyes gleaming with enjoyment.

'Perhaps we should discuss this,' he said.

'Mmm, I'd like that. But you know what?'

'What?' he asked with misgiving.

'You're acting in exactly the kind of he-man style that they're imagining.'

'Oh, *hell*!'

He rolled off her but she immediately followed until she'd rolled on top of him, thanking her lucky stars that the bed was wide enough for this kind of frolicking.

'Now it's my turn to be the he-man,' she informed him.

'I didn't think it worked that way.'

'It does when I do it.'

He gave her his wickedest look. 'I'm at your mercy, dragon lady,' he said with relish.

'You'd better believe it.'

She began to work on his shirt buttons, opening them swiftly until she could run her hands over his chest. By the violent tremors that went through him she could tell that he loved it, but he made no move to do the same for her.

'Are you going to just lie there?' she demanded indignantly.

'What else can I do? I am but a mere wimp, awaiting orders.'

'Well,' she said, breathing hard, 'my orders are for you to go into action.'

'Right!'

One swift, forceful movement was enough to demolish the front of her dress. Then she was on her back, having the rest of her clothes ripped away.

'To hear is to obey,' he murmured, tossing aside his own clothes and settling on top of her.

They fought it out, laughing, loving, challenging, bickering amiably, then doing it all again until they fell asleep in each other's arms, happy and exhausted.

It was a good night.

Now and then the boat stopped and everyone went ashore for an excursion to a temple, or to view one of the famous Three Gorges dams. Lang and Olivia joined these expeditions but they were always glad to get back on board.

In the privacy of their suite they could enjoy not merely love-making but talk. To both of them it was a special joy that their pleasure in each other was not confined to passion. Huddled close, they could explore hearts and minds in sleepy content.

Olivia found herself talking about her fractured life as she'd never done before, except with Norah.

'You said once that I was my mother's mother, and you were right. My parents are just like a couple of kids. It can seem charming, until you see all the people they've let down.'

'Mostly you,' Lang said tenderly.

'Yes, but there's a queue that stretches behind me—Tony, my mother's second husband, her step-children by that marriage, her child by Tony—my half-brother. He's about fourteen now and beginning to realise what she's like. He calls me sometimes for advice. I do my best, but I've never told him the worst she's capable of.'

She fell silent. At last Lang said, 'Tell me, if you can.'

'I was about twelve. It was December and I was getting all excited about Christmas. I was staying with Norah, but Dad and I were going to Paris together. I got ready, everything packed, and waited for him. When he was late I went outside and sat on the wall, looking for his car to appear at the end of the road, but he didn't come.

'Norah called him, but all she got was the answer machine. We tried his mobile phone but it was switched off. I suppose I knew in my heart that he wasn't coming, but I wouldn't face it. At last, hours later, he called to see if I was having a great time with my mother. I said, "But I'm supposed to be with you." Then it all came out about Evadne, his new girlfriend. She'd begged him to take her to Paris instead of me, and been very persuasive, so he'd left a message on my mother's phone to say she'd have to have me. He seemed terribly surprised that she hadn't turned up.'

Lang swore violently and rolled over away from her, his hands over his face. Then he rolled back and took her in his arms. 'I will kill him,' he muttered over and over. 'Don't ever let me meet your father or I will kill him. Hold onto me—hold me.'

It felt so good to embrace him, to bury her head

against his shoulder and blot out everything else, as though he had it in his power to put the world right.

'So you had to spend Christmas with your mother?' he said at last.

'Oh, no, she didn't get his message until she'd left to spend Christmas with her new boyfriend—at least, she said she didn't. So neither of them came for me and I spent Christmas with Norah.'

He seized her again and this time it was he who hid his face in her shoulder, as though her pain was unbearable to him.

'How did you survive?' he murmured.

'Part of me didn't. I learned not to trust people, especially when they talked about their feelings. I thought Andy was different, but he was just the same.'

'Was he the only one?'

'You mean, have I had other boyfriends? Oh, yes. I dipped my toe in the water a few times, but only my toe. I always got cautious before I went too far. It doesn't take much to turn me back into that little girl sitting on the wall, watching for someone who never appeared. In my heart—' she shuddered '—I always know that's going to happen.'

'Never,' he said violently. 'Never, do you hear me? I'm yours for life. Or at least for as long as you want me. No, don't answer.' He laid a swift hand over her lips. 'You can't promise life, not yet. I know that. But I'll be patient. Just remember that I'm always here.'

'Always,' she murmured longingly.

Always? queried the voice in her head. If only.

But held in his arms she could believe in anything, and she clung to him in desperate hope.

CHAPTER NINE

SOMETIMES he teased her about her preference for good sense.

'If I really believed in good sense I'd never have come anywhere near you,' she said indignantly.

'You're trying to reform me. I realised that ages ago.'

'I'm not having much luck, am I? Sometimes I doubt myself. You know those marvellous roofs you see on old buildings, the ones that curve up at the corners? I read that it dates back to a Buddhist belief about evil residing in straight lines, so they should be avoided if possible.

'But another book talked about architecture and rainfall, and how the curve was precisely calculated to give maximum benefit to the building. I hated that. I like the Buddhist interpretation much better.'

Lang's response was to lift Ming Zhi from beside the bed, and address Olivia severely.

'You're slipping. That kind of sentimentality isn't what I engaged you for.'

They laughed, cocooned in the safe refuge they offered each other. Their laughter ended in passion.

Another time Olivia recalled the night she'd met the Langs, and had seen him in the context of both his families.

'They say a picture's worth a thousand words,' she murmured. 'You told me how out of place you felt with your English family, but it only became real when I saw the photograph of you all together. You looked exactly like them, but I could still see you were a fish out of water.'

'That's putting it mildly,' he said. 'But, looking back, I feel sorry for them.'

'Sorry for *them*?'

'I know I was difficult. In some ways I'm not a very nice character. You said I looked like a misfit with them, and that was how I felt. But in my mind it was they who were the misfits, and I was the one who'd got it right, which isn't very amiable in a fifteen-year-old boy.'

'No, but it *is* very typical of fifteen-year-old boys,' she riposted. 'So you were a grumpy adolescent—join the club.'

'That's one way of looking at it,' he said with a self-mocking smile. 'The other way is that I'm stubborn, inflexible and set on my own way. Once

I want something I won't give up. Everyone else becomes the victim.' He tightened his arms around her. 'As you have cause to know.'

'Mmm, I'm not complaining.'

'Good, because I've got you and I'm going to keep you.'

'Do I get a say about that?' she teased.

'Nope, you have nothing to say about it. You belong to me, understand?'

She couldn't resist saying, 'You mean, like Jaio belonged to the Emperor Qin?'

'No way. She escaped. You'll never escape me.'

'What, no gallant warrior to ride to my rescue?'

'The man who could take you away from me hasn't been born.'

'What happened to being patient and letting me decide in my own time?'

'That was then. This is now.'

She chuckled. 'That's all right, then. I'll forgive you if you're a bit overbearing, or even a lot overbearing. Which you most definitely will be. Anything else you want to warn me about?'

He kissed her, adding thoughtfully, 'Plenty. Take my career—I want to be the best. I have to be the best, whatever it means.'

'This job that's coming up?'

'Yes. I've set my heart on it.'

'But you've only been here three years. Aren't you rushing it?'

'I know the other likely candidates and they don't worry me. Besides, the present incumbent hasn't retired yet, and probably won't for another year. I'll be patient until then.'

The unconscious arrogance of that 'I'll be patient' told her he was speaking the truth about himself. He was still the man who'd won her heart, gentle, charming, humorous. But she was learning that his apparent diffidence masked a confidence and determination so implacable that he himself was made uneasy by it. He flinched from it, tried to disguise it, but it was the unalterable truth.

As long as he was determined to keep her with him, she was happy to live with it.

Life wasn't entirely smooth. On the night after the talent contest there was a dance for the passengers. Wanting to dazzle him, Olivia did herself up to the nines, including wearing one of the dresses she'd bought at the last minute before their departure. It was another *cheongsam*, this time in black satin embroidered with silver, and even more alluring than the last, which made Lang eye her wryly.

'You wouldn't be trying to make me jealous by any chance, would you?' he murmured.

'Think I couldn't?'

'We'll have to see.'

She soon realised her mistake. The events of the night before had given Lang a reputation guaranteed to fascinate everyone there. The girls lined up to dance with him. Their men lined up to prevent them. When they couldn't do that they danced with Olivia instead, hoping to aggravate him.

But they had mistaken their man, as Olivia could have told them. Lang seemed oblivious to everything except the succession of women in his arms, which was obviously the clever way to react, even if she did find it personally aggravating.

Watching him from a slight distance, she could admire his graceful, athletic movements. With her imagination heightened to fever pitch she mentally undressed him, feeling those same movements against her, not dancing but loving her powerfully. Her own dancing became more erotic, something she couldn't have controlled if she'd tried. And she wasn't trying.

Just once he looked directly at her and their gazes locked in the perfect comprehension that so often united them. He was doing the same as she, teasing and enticing until they were ready to haul each other off the floor and into bed. Excitement streamed through her, making every nerve tingle with anticipatory pleasure. If only he would make his move soon.

Meaning to urge him along, she allowed herself

a little extra wiggle. The result was all she hoped. Lang bid his partner a hasty goodbye, made it across the floor at top speed and hoisted her into his arms.

'You've gone too far,' he said firmly.

'I hope so. Better too far than not far enough,' she said, reminding him of his own words in the zoo.

By this time they were halfway down the corridor. When they reached the door of their suite, Olivia opened it and Lang kicked it shut behind them. When he tossed her onto the bed she reached up to undo the *cheongsam*.

'No,' he said, removing her hands. 'That's my job.'

'Then get on with it,' she ordered him, edgy with frustration.

He needed no further urging. By the time he'd finished the dress was in tatters on the floor, followed by her underwear. When they were both naked he drew back, breathing heavily, kneeling beside her on the bed. His arousal was hard, almost violent, yet he had the control to stop there, looking down at her with a glint in his eyes that was new.

'You promised to throw me over your shoulder,' she reproached him. 'What happened?'

'I'm a gentleman,' he said in a rasping breath.

'Nah, you're a coward. If you'd kept me waiting any longer, I'd have thrown you over *my* shoulder.'

'That's because you're no lady.' He lay down

beside her until his lips were against her ear. 'I watched you dancing all night, and believe me you are *no* lady.'

She gave a sigh of deep contentment. 'I'm glad you realise that.'

His hands were touching her, but differently from before. The movements were fiercer, more purposeful, as though something that had been holding him back had disappeared, releasing him. Now he loved her with a driving urgency, with power, as well as skill, conquering and taking where once he would have waited for her to give.

At the end she was exhausted but triumphant. She'd always suspected that this forceful arrogance was one of the mysteries that lay behind his mild manners, and there was deep satisfaction in having tempted it out at last.

'Are you all right?' he asked quietly. 'I hadn't meant to be quite so—adventurous.'

The other Lang was back, the quiet one with perfect manners. But she'd seen beyond him now, and she liked what she'd discovered.

'Perhaps we should try it that way a few more times,' she said with a contented smile. 'I rather enjoy not being a lady.'

He laughed. 'Were you actually trying to make me jealous tonight?'

'I suppose I was,' she said in a pensive voice. 'But you did quite a bit yourself.'

'You couldn't expect me to ignore your challenge.'

'But it's not fair. I have so much more to be jealous of than you.'

'You think I'm not jealous of Andy?'

'Who? Oh, him. You shouldn't be. You know all about him, and I know nothing about your love life—unless you expect me to believe you've lived like a monk.'

She thought he paused a little before saying lightly, 'Certainly not. I told you about Becky Renton—perhaps not everything, but—'

'Spare me the details of what happened behind the bicycle sheds at school. I don't even want to know about the girls you took to the Dancing Dragon.'

'I explained.'

'Yes, I remember your explanation—very carefully edited, which was probably wise of you.'

He regarded her wryly. 'Do you want chapter and verse?'

Warning bells went off in her mind. This was straying into dangerous territory.

He was lying on his back with Olivia on her stomach beside him with a clear view of his face and its suddenly withdrawn look. Two instincts warred within her. She was curious about his life yet reluctant to sound like a jealous nag.

Let it go, she thought. She'd just had the clearest demonstration of what she was to him.

'Of course I don't want chapter and verse,' she said firmly. 'I know you must have played the field. It would worry me more if you hadn't.'

She put an arm about his neck and lay over him, her face against his shoulder, feeling him curve his arm to hold her more closely.

'There is one I'd like to tell you about,' he said at last. 'So that there are no secrets between us.'

'All right. Go on.' Now the moment was here she only wanted to back away, but it was too late.

'I was like you for a long time,' he said. 'I never let myself get too far into a relationship. I knew where I was heading and I didn't want anything to get in the way. But a few months before I left England I fell in love with a girl called Natalie.

'Everything seemed perfect. We planned to get married and come to China together. But one day I found her looking through advertisements for houses, hoping to buy one for us to live in. When I reminded her about China, she laughed and said, "Isn't it time to be realistic?"

'I understood then that she'd never really meant to come with me. She'd thought of it as nonsense that I'd get over. When she realised that I was serious, she became angry. She forced me to choose between her and China, and so—' He paused. 'And so we said goodbye.'

Olivia had raised herself so that she could look down at him. He turned his head to look at her, and now she wished she could read what was in his eyes.

'Did you ever regret letting her go?' She had to ask, although she feared the answer.

'She'd been deceiving me all that time, keeping a distance between us when I'd thought we were so close. Our minds would always have been apart.'

'But if you loved her—it's not just minds, is it?'

He glanced at her naked body leaning over him, the beautiful breasts hanging down so that the nipples touched him, and he caressed them gently.

'No,' he said softly, 'it's not just minds. But you and I have everything—minds, as well as hearts and bodies. Have you not felt that?'

'Yes, from the first moment.'

'You would never hide your thoughts from me, or I from you. I didn't tell you about Natalie before because I was afraid you would misunderstand and think it had more importance than it has.'

'And how much does it have?'

'Some, for a while. But now none at all. She married someone else last year, and I'm glad for her. If we'd married it would have been a disaster, because we would each have wanted something the other could never give. There's nothing there to make you jealous. The wisest thing I ever did was to wait for you.'

She lay down against him, reassured and content. It wasn't until the last moment that it occurred to her that there was something ominous in the story, but before she could think of it she was asleep.

Only one person was welcome in their secret world, and that was Norah.

The boat had a computer link-up and Olivia had brought her laptop. Now they both enjoyed going online to her. She and Lang would embark on a chat as though taking up where they'd left off only a few minutes before. Norah liked him as she had never liked Andy, Olivia realised.

He talked about the Yangtze, describing the view from the deck until her eyes shone.

'Oh, that must have been so marvellous!' she exclaimed. 'What a sight!'

'Perhaps you'll see it yourself one day,' he suggested.

'That would be lovely, but I'm old now. I don't think there are any long journeys for me.'

'Who knows what the future holds?' Lang said mysteriously.

Listening to this, Olivia wondered if she was

reading too much into a few words, but they seemed to lead in only one direction. If she and Lang were to choose a life together, she would have to move permanently to China. His life here was too settled to allow any doubt.

For just a little longer they could live in this private universe where the real world was set at a distance. But soon the practical decisions would have to be made.

They said goodnight and hung up. Lang was regarding her with a question in his eyes.

'Something troubling you?'

'I was just wondering about Norah. She's very old, and when you talk of her coming here...'

'She's not too old for China. Old people get treated very well here, better than in many other countries.'

'Yes, I know, but that long air-journey.'

'Can be made a lot more comfortable with an upgrade.' He gave her a conspiratorial smile, reminding her that the word had a special significance for them. 'We just buy her a ticket in business class, where she can travel in comfort, stretch out and go to sleep. I think she'd like it here.'

'Lang, what are you saying?'

'I'm just looking ahead, down many different roads, but they all lead to you, my love. Let it happen as it will.'

Yes, she thought, that was the way. Fate, something she'd never believed in before, but which now seemed the only way.

Yet the flight arrangements he'd mentioned showed that he'd been thinking about this in detail, planning for the day.

He partially explained the mystery as they lay together later.

'It comes from belonging to two different cultures,' he said sleepily. 'One side of me believes in fate and destiny, good luck, bad luck, being touched by another world we can't control. The other side makes graphs and looks up flight timetables.'

'Which side of you is which?'

'They're mixed up. Both cultures have both aspects, but they speak with different accents. Sometimes I tell myself how completely I belong here. I love my Chinese family.'

'And they love you dearly too. Biyu talked of you being "a little bit English" as though that bit doesn't matter at all next to your Chinese quarter. It must be wonderful to be so completely accepted.'

A slight shadow came over Lang's face.

'What is it?' Olivia asked. 'Have I said something wrong?'

'No, it's just that you speak of them accepting me.'

'But they do, that's obvious.'

'I know it looks like that, and I'm probably imagining that the acceptance isn't complete. I simply have this feeling that they're holding back just a little.'

'But why?'

'I don't know. All I can tell you is that I feel they're waiting for me to do something, or say something. But I don't know what it is.'

'I think you're wrong. They're not holding back at all. They're so proud of you, and they're especially proud that you came here and chose them. Biyu did this.' She tapped her breast. 'And she said, "In here, he is one of us".'

'She actually said that?' There was something touchingly boyish in his eagerness.

'She actually said that. So doesn't that prove you're accepted?'

'Maybe, but I don't think even they know that something doesn't fit.'

'Then you have to be patient,' Olivia said. 'It'll happen naturally, and you'll all know by instinct.'

'I didn't think you believed in trusting your instinct.'

'But it's not *my* instinct we're talking about.'

'Perhaps it is. I think that whatever we seem to be talking about we're also finding out about each other—and about ourselves.'

'Yes, it's alarming when you start to discover that you're not the person you thought you were,' she agreed.

'What have you learned about yourself?' he murmured, his mouth close to hers.

'Things that alarm me. Things that I'm not sure I want to learn.'

'Tell me about them.'

'I'm just not the person I thought I was—but, if I'm not, then who am I?'

'Does it matter?'

'Of course it matters. What a question!'

'I'm serious. Why do you have to know who you are? It's enough that you *are*. And, besides, I know you. You're a dragon lady—wild, brave, inventive, everything that's powerful and good.'

'To you, yes. But that would mean putting myself entirely in your hands.'

'Don't you trust me that much?'

'It's not that, it's just—I don't know.'

'Believe me, I know what it's like to put yourself in the hands of the woman you love and to realise that, if she understands you, it doesn't matter whether you understand yourself because she's wiser than you are.'

He might have been talking about Natalie, but the warmth in his eyes told her what he really meant.

'Perhaps you should be careful,' she whispered. 'Who knows if I can really be trusted that much?'

'I do,' he said at once. 'I'd trust you with my life, with my heart, soul and all my future.'

'But we've known each other such a little time.'

'We've known each other for over two-thousand years,' he said. 'Ever since the moment I caught a glimpse of your face and knew that I'd gladly give up everything else in my life in order to be with you.'

'Is that you talking?' she asked in wonder. 'Or Renshu?'

'Ah!' he said with satisfaction. 'I said you understood me. Yes, I'm Renshu, and so is every man who's ever loved as much as I do. And I know one thing—I can't be without you. You must stay with me for ever or my life will be nothing.

'I know you can't abandon Norah, but I don't ask you to. She has been your mother, and from now on she will be mine too. She'll be happy in China, I'll make sure of that. Don't you think I can?'

'I think you can do anything you set your mind to,' she said in wonder.

'Does that mean yes?'

'Yes, yes, *yes*!'

Flinging her arms about him, she hugged him with wild joy and he hugged her back powerfully. When they drew back to behold each other's faces she saw that his was full of mischief.

'I was so afraid you'd refuse me,' he said meekly.

'Liar, liar! You never thought that for a moment,' she cried, thumping him. 'You're the most conceited devil that ever lived.'

'Only because you make me conceited,' he defended himself, laughing. 'If you love me, how can I not have a good opinion of myself? I merely bow to the dragon lady's superior good sense. Ow! That hurt!' He rubbed his thigh where she'd landed a lucky slap.

'I never said I loved you,' she riposted. 'I'm marrying you out of pity. No— Ah, wait!' Her laughter died as something occurred to her. 'You never actually mentioned marriage, did you?'

'I didn't think it needed mentioning. It has to be marriage. Of course, I'd really prefer to keep you as a concubine— No, no, I give in!' He fended off a renewed attack, securing her arms and keeping her close for safety. 'You don't think Tao and Biyu and the others would let me deprive them of a wedding, do you?'

'Shall we go back to Beijing and tell everyone?'

'Not just yet. Let's go off on our own for a while. You once mentioned Shanghai? Let's go there. But, in the meantime, let's dress for dinner. Put on your glad rags because you're going to enjoy tonight.'

CHAPTER TEN

As THEY were having dinner he explained what he'd meant. 'After this we'll go back to the little theatre,' he said.

'Not another talent contest, please!'

'No, they're doing a play with music. It's based on a fable that goes back centuries, and it's known as the Chinese *Romeo and Juliet*.'

'Star-crossed lovers?'

'That's right. He was poor, her family was rich. When they couldn't marry, he died of a broken heart, but she went to his tomb and— Well, wait and see.'

When dinner was over they slipped into place, securing a table near the stage. Gradually the lights went down and plaintive music filled the air. Zhu Yingtai, a beautiful young girl, appeared with her family, pleading with them for the right to study. They were shocked at this unladylike behaviour, but finally let her go to college disguised as a man. She sang of her joy:

'Other women dream of husbands,
But I do not seek a husband.
I choose freedom.'

As the scene changed Lang whispered provocatively to Olivia, 'She's looking forward to a life of learning and independence, with no male complications. I know you'll approve.'

She smiled. It seemed such a long time since she'd been that woman, and the man who'd released her from her cage was sitting so close that she could feel his warmth mingling with another kind of warmth that was part memory, part anticipation.

In the next scene Zhu Yingtai, now dressed as a man, met Liang Shanbo and they became fellow students. They grew close, singing about their deep friendship.

'Our hearts beat together.
All is understood between us.'

'And yet he doesn't suspect that she's a woman?' Olivia mused.

'Perhaps friendship is also part of love,' Lang murmured. 'If they'd been able to marry, the fact that they could confide in each other might have sustained them through the years, making them strong while other couples fell apart.'

His face was very close to hers, his eyes glowing with a message he knew she could understand without words. She nodded slowly.

At last Zhu Yingtai revealed her true identity and they declared their love, but it was in vain. Liang Shanbo was poor. Her parents betrothed her to a rich man.

He sang a plaintive ballad, full of heartbreak, saying that his life was nothing without his beloved. Then he lay down and quietly died.

The day of Zhu Yingtai's wedding dawned. She too sang, longing for death to reunite her with the man she loved. On the way to the ceremony she stopped beside her lover's tomb, crying out her longing for them to be together.

Olivia held her breath. For some reason what would happen next mattered to her.

The music swelled. The tomb doors opened. Zhu Yingtai threw up her arms in ecstatic gratitude and walked triumphantly inside.

The lights dimmed, except for one brilliant beam over the tomb. From somewhere overhead a hologram was projected into the light, and two large butterflies came into view. They hovered for a moment before flying off together into the darkness.

These were the souls of the lovers, now united for ever. The audience gasped, then applauded ecstatically. The lights came up and Olivia hastily dried her eyes.

All about them people were exclaiming with appreciation. Lang and Olivia quietly slipped away and went up on deck.

'Did I understand the end properly?' she asked as they strolled hand in hand. 'The butterflies were the lovers, and now they'll always be together?'

'That's right.'

She stopped and looked up at the moon. No full moon tonight, but a crescent hanging in the sky. Lang followed her gaze.

'According to Meihui,' he said, 'the two butterflies didn't only signify reunion in death, but eternal fidelity in life also. She said there were so many different stage versions all over China that one or other was always being performed. When I came here, almost the first thing I did was to find a performance, to see if it spoke to me in her voice, and it did. I was so glad it was on here tonight, so that I could show it to you.'

'Butterflies,' she mused. 'Flying away together for eternity. What a lovely thought!'

'Eternity,' he echoed. 'That's what I want with you, if it's what you want.'

'It's all I shall ever want,' she told him passionately.

'Then we have everything. Let's go inside.'

'We can go on travelling for another couple of weeks,' Lang said next morning. 'And then it'll be back to Beijing to plan the wedding.'

'And that's going to take a lot of planning,' Olivia mused.

'Nonsense, we just give Biyu the date and leave everything to her. In fact, why don't we just let her choose the date?'

'Good idea. She'll be better at planning it than I will.'

Biyu thought so too. In a feverish telephone call, she tried to make them return at once and plunge into arrangements. It took all Lang's strength to resist, and when he hung up Olivia had to take drastic steps to restore his energy. That distracted them so long that they got behind with their packing and nearly weren't ready when the boat docked at Yichang.

From there they took a plane to Shangai on the coast. During the flight, they planned out the rest of their trip.

'We could go to Chengdu and see the panda sanctuary,' he said. 'I've got some more relatives up there, and I'd like them to meet you. But let's enjoy Shanghai first.'

It was a revelation, an ultra-modern, bustling city where almost every inch seemed to be neon-lit. On the first night they took a boat down the river, gazing up at the skyscrapers adorned with multi-coloured lights. Then they escaped to their hotel room on the thirty-fifth floor and watched from the window.

'I'm dizzy being up so high,' she murmured, leaning back against him.

'I'm dizzy too,' he whispered against her neck. 'But it's not from the height.'

She chuckled but didn't move, even when he drew his lips across the skin below her ear, although it sent delicious tremors through her.

'Come to bed,' he urged.

'Can't you just let a girl enjoy the view?'

'No,' he said firmly, sweeping her up and carrying her to the huge bed, where she forgot all about skyscrapers and neon lights.

They slept late, rose late and sauntered out, meaning to do some serious educational sightsee-ing. They ended up in a theatre where motorbike riders diced with death, crossing each other's path within inches at high speed.

'Well, I've learned something,' she remarked as they walked slowly back to the hotel. 'I've learned never to get on a motorbike.'

They had the elevator to themselves and kissed all the way to the thirty-fifth floor, their minds running ahead to the pleasures to come.

But as they reached their room Lang's mobile phone began to buzz. Groaning, he answered, and Olivia saw him grow instantly alert. The next moment he swung away from her, as though she had no part of what was happening, and went to stand by the window.

He was talking too rapidly for her to follow, and his whole body was alive with excitement. When he hung up, he looked as though he was lit from within.

'That's it!' he cried. 'I knew it must happen some time.'

He hurled himself on the bed and lay back with his hands behind his head, the picture of triumph. Then he saw her regarding him, puzzled, and opened his arms to her. She went into them and nearly had the breath squeezed out of her.

'What's happened?' she gasped, laughing.

'That vacancy for a consultant has come up at the hospital!' he cried exultantly. 'It's a brilliant opportunity. Just what I've been waiting for.'

'That's wonderful. Who called you?'

'Another doctor, a friend who knows how badly I want this. He's put my name forward, and he called to tell me when the interviews start.'

'So we have to go back now,' she said, trying not to sound too disappointed.

'No, nothing's going to happen until next week. We can have another couple of days. And then...' He sighed. 'Back to the real world.'

'But the real world is going to be wonderful,' she reminded him. 'You're going to be a great consultant, and in a few years you'll be in charge of the whole hospital.'

'I hope so. If you only knew how much I hope so. I want it so much it scares me.'

That night was different. They made love and slept close as always, but when Olivia awoke in the small hours she saw him standing at the window looking out, so preoccupied that he never once looked back at the bed.

She wondered where he was now, inside his mind, and concluded that wherever it was she wasn't there with him. It was the first shadow on their relationship, only a tiny one, but perceptible.

Next day he seemed preoccupied over breakfast, and she said little, understanding that he would wish to mull over the situation that was opening up to him. They went out on a brief shopping-expedition, but over lunch he suddenly left her alone and was away for nearly an hour. Returning, he apologised profusely, but didn't say where he'd been. Sadly, she realised that part of him was already returning to 'the real world', where she seemed to live on the margins.

Or did she live anywhere at all? Had she, in the end, been nothing but a holiday romance? Lang had spoken of marriage and eternity, but that was before he'd been offered the chance of the thing he admitted he wanted more than anything in the world.

Suddenly she was in darkness, stumbling about an alien universe. She had survived Andy's betrayal. She knew she wouldn't survive Lang's.

But the moment of doubt passed, and that evening her fears were eased when Lang suggested talking to Norah.

In a moment they were online, and there was Norah's face, beaming at them.

'Hello, darling! And, Lang—is that you I see?'

'Hello, Norah,' he said, seating himself on the bed next to Olivia, before the little camera. 'How are you?'

'Better than ever since my gifts arrived. Look.'

She held up the tiny figurine of a terracotta warrior in one hand, and a book in the other.

'The postman delivered them this morning,' she bubbled. 'It was so kind of you.'

He told her about Biyu and the wedding plans.

'As soon as we've set the date we'll arrange your flight out here,' he told her.

For a moment Olivia thought a faint shadow

crossed Norah's face, but it was gone too quickly for her to be sure. It might have been a trick of the camera.

'What kind of a wedding are you going to have?' Norah wanted to know.

Lang talked at length, describing in detail what would probably happen and the part he expected her to play in it. She giggled and called him a cheeky young devil, which seemed to please him.

'Hey, can I get a word in edgeways?' Olivia protested. 'How about saying something about my new dress?'

'It's very pretty, dear.'

'I chose it,' Lang put in.

'Of course you did. Olivia's dress sense was always a little wayward.'

'Oi!' Olivia cried.

'Well, it's true, darling. But Lang has wonderful taste. You should always listen to him.'

'I'll remind her of that,' Lang said gravely.

'Oi!' Olivia said again, nudging him in the ribs with her elbow. He gave an exaggerated wince, which made Norah laugh more than ever.

'I'm so glad you're having a wonderful time,' she said. 'You look ever so much better. I was becoming afraid for you, but not any more.'

'Don't be afraid for her,' Lang said, suddenly

serious. He slipped his arm around Olivia in such a way that Norah could see it.

'I never will again,' she said. 'Darling, you be good to him. He's one in a million.'

'I know,' Olivia replied, gazing back at the old woman with love. Norah beamed back, their understanding as perfect as ever.

'Now I've got some marvellous news to tell you,' Lang said.

'More marvellous news? As well as your marriage? Tell, tell.'

'I've had a call from—'

He stopped as a terrible change came over Norah. Her smile faded abruptly and she gave a choking sound. Aghast, they watched as she clutched her throat and heaved in distress.

'Norah!' Olivia cried, reaching out frantically to the screen. But Norah was five thousand miles away. 'Oh, heavens, what's happening to her?'

'I think she's having a heart attack,' Lang said.

'A heart attack?' Olivia echoed in horror. 'Oh, no, it can't be!'

'I'm afraid it is,' he said tersely, not taking his eyes from the screen. 'Norah—can you hear me?'

Norah couldn't speak, but she managed to nod.

'Don't fight it,' Lang told her. 'Try to take deep, slow breaths until the ambulance reaches you.'

Olivia was dialling her mobile phone.

'I'm calling her neighbour in the apartment downstairs,' she said. 'Hello, Jack, it's Olivia. Norah's having a heart attack—can you—? Norah, Jack says he's on his way.'

'Can he get in?' Lang asked.

'Yes, they've each got a key to the other's place so that they can keep an eye on each other. There he is.'

They could see Jack on the screen now, an elderly man but still full of vigour. He reached for Norah's phone, dialling for the ambulance.

'It's on its way,' he said at last to Olivia.

'Thank you,' she wept.

By now Norah was lying back on the pillow, not moving. They saw Jack try to rouse her, but she lay terrifyingly still.

'She's passed out,' Jack said desperately. *'What can I do?'*

'Don't panic,' Lang said firmly. 'I'm a doctor, do as I say. Place two fingers against her throat to check for a pulse.'

Jack did so, but wailed, 'I can't feel anything, and she's stopped breathing. Oh, dear God, she's dead!'

'No!' Olivia screamed.

'Don't panic, either of you,' Lang said sternly. 'She isn't dead, but she's had a cardiac arrest. Jack, we've got to get her heart started again. First raise her legs about eighteen inches, to help blood flow back to the heart.'

They both watched as Jack put a couple of pillows under Norah's feet, then looked back at the screen for further instructions.

'Place the palm of your hand flat on her chest just over the lower part of her breast bone,' Lang continued. 'Then press down in a pumping motion. Use the other hand, as well, to give extra power—that's it! Excellent.'

'But is it working?' Olivia whispered.

'Don't disturb him,' Lang advised.

As they watched, Norah made a slight movement. Jack gave a yell of triumph.

'The medics should be here soon,' he said. 'I left the main door open so that they could—Here they are.'

Two ambulance crew burst in, armed with equipment, confidently taking over. One of them asked Jack what he'd done, then nodded in approval.

'Well done,' he said. 'She was lucky to have you.'

As they moved Norah onto the stretcher, Jack addressed the screen.

'I'm going to the hospital with her,' he said. 'I'll call you when I know something.'

'Give her my love,' Olivia begged. 'Tell her I'll be there soon. And, Jack, thank you for everything.'

'It's not me you should thank, it's him,' he said gruffly, and the screen went dead.

'He's right,' she whispered. 'If she lives, you did it.'

'Of course she will live,' Lang insisted.

'I shouldn't have left her. She's old and frail. I've stayed away too long.'

'But she wanted you to. Every time I've seen her she's been encouraging you, smiling.'

'Yes, because she's sweet and generous. She must have smiled on purpose to make me think she was all right. She was thinking of me, but I should have been thinking of her.'

'Olivia, my darling, stop blaming yourself. You're right, she is generous. She knew that you needed your freedom and she gave it to you. Accept her generosity.'

'I know you're right, but—'

She could say no more. Grief overwhelmed her and she sobbed helplessly. Lang's arms went around her, holding her close, offering her all the comfort in his power.

Many times in the past he'd held her with passion, letting her know that she could bring his body alive, as he could hers. But now there was only strength and tenderness, giving without taking, all the warmth and compassion of his nature offered in her service.

She stopped weeping at last, because the strength had drained out of her. Normally so decisive, she now found herself floundering.

'Start your packing,' he told her gently, 'and I'll call the airport.'

An hour later they were on their way. Lang had found a flight to London for her, and one to Beijing for himself. When she had checked in, they sat in silence, holding hands, trying to come to terms with what had happened. One moment their joyous life had seemed set to last for ever. The next, without warning, it was all over. The speed with which light had turned to darkness left her reeling.

And yet, what had I expected? she asked herself. *We were always fooling ourselves about bringing Norah to China. I have to go to England and his life is here.*

How bitter was the irony! The woman who'd been so sure she could command her own fate had been swept away by a tide of love whose strength she was only beginning to appreciate now that it was slipping away from her.

'I've got something for you,' Lang said. 'I bought it to give you as a symbol of our coming marriage.'

'Oh, no,' she begged. 'Don't say that. I can't bear it. How can we ever marry?'

'I don't know,' he said sombrely. 'I only know that somehow we must. Don't you feel that too?'

'Yes. Yes, I do. But how can we?'

'I had hoped that we might make our home in China and Norah could come here and live with us. I still hope for that. She will recover in time, and all will be well. We have only to be patient.'

She looked at him with desperate eyes, longing to believe that it could be that easy, but she was full of fear.

'We must never give up hope,' Lang persisted. 'Don't you know that whatever happens some day, somehow, we must be together?'

'I want to think so, but how can we? I don't know how long I'll be gone, perhaps always.'

'However long it is,' he said, taking her hands between his, 'it will happen at last. There will be nobody else for me. So in the end we must find each other again, because otherwise I shall spend all my life alone. Now I've known you, there could never be anyone else.'

'You make it sound so simple,' she said huskily.

'No, I make it sound possible, because it is. That's why I want you to take this.'

He drew out a small box and placed it in her hands. Opening it, Olivia saw a brooch in the shape of a dainty, silver butterfly: the sign of eternal love and lifelong fidelity.

'I bought it yesterday, when I was gone for that time,' he said. 'I've been waiting for the right moment to give it to you, but I never thought it would be like this. Wear it and never forget that we belong together.'

'I will wear it always,' she promised.

Overhead a loudspeaker blared.

'They're calling your flight,' he said. 'Goodbye—for now.'

'For now,' she repeated.

He took her into his arms. 'Remember me,' he begged.

'Always. Just a few more moments…' She kissed him again and again.

'You must go—you must go.' But still he held onto her.

The call came again.

'Oh, God, it's so far away!' she wept. 'When will we see each other again?'

'We will,' he said fiercely. 'Somehow we'll find a way. We must hold onto that thought.'

But even as he said it there were tears on his cheeks, and now she could see that his despair was as great as her own.

The crowd was moving now, carrying her away from him. In agony she watched him grow smaller, fading, until the distance seemed to swallow him up and only his hand was still visible, faintly waving.

The flight from Shanghai to London was

thirteen hours. During the interminable time Olivia drifted in and out of sleep, pursued by uneasy dreams. Norah was there sometimes, laughing and strong as in the old days, then lying still. Lang was there too, his face anguished as he bid her farewell.

She managed to get a little restless sleep, but it was tormented by ghosts. There was Norah, as she'd seen her on-screen only a few hours ago, looking dismayed at the thought of the flight to China. Now Olivia realised that she hadn't imagined it. Norah had known she wasn't well, and she'd hidden it.

From beneath her closed eyes, tears streamed down Olivia's face.

Jack was waiting for her at the airport, his face haggard.

'She's in Intensive Care,' he said. 'She was alive when I left her an hour ago, but she's bad, really bad.'

'Then I'll get there fast.'

'Shall I take your bags home with me?' he offered. 'I expect you'll want to move into Norah's place.'

Until that moment it hadn't dawned on her that she had nowhere to go. She thanked him and hurried to the hospital.

Once there, she ran the last few steps to Inten-

sive Care, her fear mounting. A nurse rose to meet
her, smiling reassurance.

'It's all right,' she said kindly. 'She's still alive.'

Alive, but only just. Olivia approached the bed
slowly, horrified at the sight of the old woman lying
as still as death attached to a multitude of tubes.

'Norah,' Olivia said urgently, hurrying to the
side of the bed. 'It's me. Can you hear me?'

The nurse produced a chair for her, saying, 'I'm
afraid she's been like that since she was brought in.'

'But she will come round soon, surely?'
Olivia pleaded.

'We must hope so,' the nurse said gently.

Olivia leaned close to Norah. It was hard to see
her face through the tubes attached to aid her
breathing, but the deathly pallor of her skin was
frighteningly clear. She seemed thinner than
before, more fragile and lined. How could she
have gone away from Norah knowing that she
was so frail?

But she hadn't known, because Norah had been
determined to prevent her knowing. During their
talks she'd laughed and chatted, apparently
without a care in the world, because to her nothing
had mattered but that Olivia should be free to go
out and explore.

Now she was dying, perhaps without regaining

consciousness, and she might never know that the person she'd loved most had returned to her.

'I'm sorry,' Olivia said huskily. 'I shouldn't have stayed away so long. Oh, darling, you did so much for me and I wasn't there for you.'

Norah's hands were lying still on the sheet. Olivia took hold of one between both of hers, hoping by this means to get through to her, but there was no reaction. Nothing. Norah didn't know she was there, and might never know.

'Please,' Olivia begged. 'Don't die without talking to me. *Please*!'

But Norah lay so still that she might already have been dead, and the only sound was the steady rhythm of the machines

Olivia laid her head down on the bed in an attitude of despair.

CHAPTER ELEVEN

SHE must have lain there for an hour, holding Norah's hand and praying desperately for a miracle.

When it finally came it was the tiniest, most fragile of miracles, just a faint squeeze, but it was enough to make Olivia weep. Somehow, through the dark mists, Norah had sensed her. She *must* believe that. She must—she must.

She awoke to the feeling of someone shaking her shoulder.

'I'm sorry,' she mumbled. 'I didn't mean to go to sleep, but jet lag…'

'I know,' the nurse said sympathetically. 'Do you mind waiting outside while we attend to her?'

Olivia almost sleepwalked into the corridor and sat down, leaning back against the wall, exhausted. Inside her head there was a howling wilderness of grief, desolation and confusion. It felt as though that was all there would ever be again.

She forced herself to think clearly. She should call her mother.

Melisande answered at once. As briefly as possible, Olivia explained what had happened and that she was at the hospital.

'Norah could die at any moment. How long will it take you to get here?'

'Get there? Oh, darling, I don't think— Besides, she's got you. Since you went to China she's talked about nothing else. You're the one she wants. Keep in touch.'

She hung up quickly.

Well, what else did I expect? Olivia asked herself bitterly.

The nurse appeared, signalling for her to come back in.

'She's opened her eyes,' she said. 'She'll be glad to see you.'

Norah's eyes were just half-open, but they lit up at the sight of Olivia.

'You came,' she whispered.

'Of course I came.'

Norah closed her eyes again, seemingly content. Olivia sat there, holding her hand for another hour until the nurse touched her on the shoulder.

'You should go home and get some rest. She's

stable now. Give me your number and I'll call you if anything changes.'

Norah's apartment was dark and chilly. Olivia stared at her suitcases which Jack had left there for her. She knew that she should make an effort to unpack, but it was too much.

With all her heart she yearned for Lang, yearned for his voice, his comforting presence, the feel of his body close to hers. He was so far away—not just in miles but in everything that counted. Suddenly it seemed impossible that she would ever see him again.

She began to wander aimlessly around the apartment, trying to understand the depths of her isolation. Less than twenty-four hours ago she'd been the happiest woman on earth. Now the ugly silence sang in her ears, perhaps for ever.

He'd promised love eternal, but what was in his mind now—her or the all-important interview for the job? She was suddenly convinced that he must have forgotten her as soon as they'd parted, drawn back to his 'real' life.

She should call him, but what was he doing at this moment? With her mind fuzzy, she couldn't work out the time difference. He might be talking to somebody vital to his career and resent her interrupting.

She took out her mobile phone and sat staring at it, feeling stupid. After a while she put it away again.

Then it shrilled at her.

'Where have you been?' came Lang's frantic voice. 'I've been waiting and waiting, thinking you'd call me as soon as you had news. When you didn't, I nearly went crazy. I started checking the flights to see if anything had happened to your plane.'

'Oh, heavens!' She wept.

'Darling, what is it? Is she dead? Tell me.'

'No, she's alive and holding on.'

She told him about her journey—her arrival and the moment when Norah had seemed to become aware of her. She hardly knew what she said. She was almost hysterical with relief that he'd reached out to her.

'So it's good news,' Lang said. 'If she's survived the first twenty-four hours, then her chances are fine. She'll be well in no time.'

'What's been happening to you?' she asked.

'I'm back in Beijing.'

'Have you done anything about the job?'

'No, it's still only dawn here. When the day starts properly I'll get to work. Then I'm going to get myself a video link so that we can talk face to face.'

'You can call me on Norah's. I'm living there for the moment.'

'Go and get some sleep now. You must be in need of it. I love you.'

'I love you,' she said wistfully.

She hung up and tumbled into bed, trying to tell herself that Norah would soon be well; Lang had seemed sure. After all, he was a doctor. But she knew in her heart that he was being too optimistic too soon. If Norah made only a partial recovery they would be faced with huge problems and she guessed that he didn't want to think about them just yet.

She went to the hospital early next day. Norah was still unconscious, but after an hour she opened her eyes. Her smile as she beheld Olivia was full of happiness.

'I thought I'd only dreamed that you were here,' she murmured.

'No, I'm here, and I'm staying to look after you until you're all right.'

'What about Lang?'

'He's fine. I've talked to him.'

'What was the marvellous news he was going to tell me?'

'There's a big job coming up and he reckons he's in line for it. He's very ambitious.'

She went on talking softly until Norah's eyes drooped again and she drifted into a normal sleep.

'Is she going to make it?' Olivia asked the nurse softly.

'The doctor thinks so. Despite her age, she's very strong. It's too soon to be certain, but it'll probably work out.'

She went home feeling more cheerful than she'd dared to hope. Norah would recover and their plans could go on as before. She *must* believe that.

The next day Lang hooked up online and she saw his face for the first time since their goodbye. The sight gave her heart a jolt. He was so near, yet so far. She gave him the nurse's words.

'What did I tell you?' he said cheerfully. 'Biyu will be delighted. She'd actually pencilled in a date for our wedding—the twenty-third of next month. When I explained about the delay, she was very put out. So was Hai. He was practically lining the fish up to be caught.'

Olivia laughed shakily.

'Tell them I'm sorry to disappoint them, and I'll be back when I can.'

How hollow those words sounded to her own ears.

'They'll be glad to hear that. Wei's fiancée is writing a new song to sing at the wedding. I've got an interview for the job next week, and someone has dropped me a private hint that my chances are good.'

'Darling, I'm so thrilled for you. It'll be everything you always wanted.'

'You know better than that,' he told her.

'Yes, I do. It's just that things look different now that we're so far apart.'

'But we aren't far apart,' he said at once. 'In here—' he tapped his breast '—you're still with me, and you always will be. Nothing has changed.'

When he talked like that it was easy to believe that things would work out well. But when they had disconnected there came the time, which she dreaded. Then the distance became not merely real but the only reality.

Inch by inch she slipped into a routine. In the morning she was a housekeeper, shopping and cleaning. In the afternoon she visited Norah, now out of Intensive Care.

In the evenings she linked up to wait for Lang to appear on-screen. It occurred to her that she was following much the same timetable Norah had followed while waiting for her to call from China. When the connection finally came it marked the beginning of her day. When it was over, she counted the hours until the next one.

With a heavy heart she realised that this was how it must have felt for Norah years ago, waiting for news of her lover overseas, until finally there was nothing left to hope for.

One day Lang didn't appear at the usual time. When he finally came online he apologised and said he'd been helping out at the hospital.

'There was an emergency and they called in all hands. I've decided to abandon the rest of my vacation and go back to work. It could be useful to be on the spot—just in case.'

'I think that's very wise,' she said cheerfully.

'It means I don't know exactly what time I'll be calling,' he said.

'It doesn't matter. I'll stay hooked up permanently so that I'm always ready.'

Which was exactly what Norah had done for her, she remembered, and the similarity made her shiver.

On the day of his interview she waited by the computer for hours and knew, as soon as she saw him, that things had gone well.

'I'm through to the next stage,' he said triumphantly. 'I have to meet the whole board next week.'

That meeting too went well, and Lang confided that several board members had spoken in complimentary terms of his work at the hospital over the last three years. He said it without apparent conceit, but she was certain that he knew exactly how good he was.

Then a problem developed. His name was Guo Daiyu, and he was brilliant, Lang told her despondently.

'He didn't hear of the job at first, but someone told him recently and he hurried to apply. He has an excellent reputation, and he's the one person who could take it away from me.'

She comforted him as best she could, but she could see that the thought of losing the prize at the last minute was appalling to him.

It was ironic, she thought as she lay staring into the darkness in the early hours. Lang talked romantically, he spoke of his family's legend of love, but beneath it he was a fiercely ambitious man who knew the value of practical things.

She still believed in his love, but she also knew that the coming struggle was going to reveal each one of them to the other in a way that might destroy them.

Now she found herself remembering the story of Natalie, the woman he'd loved but had given up because she'd threatened to divert him from his chosen path. That path had included China and his professional ambition, and nothing would be allowed to stand in the way. Nothing. That was the message, clear and simple.

Then something happened. It was stupid, incongruous and even amusing in a faintly hysterical way, and it cast another light on the turn her life was taking.

After some nagging on Olivia's part, her parents visited Norah in hospital. They giggled a lot, said the right things and left as soon as possible.

Her father seemed faintly embarrassed to see her, but that was par for the course. He muttered something about how she must be short of money, pressed a cheque into her hand and departed, confident of having done his fatherly duty.

The cheque was large enough to make Olivia stare, and since she was indeed short of money she accepted it thankfully, if wryly. But she wondered what was going on.

She found out when her mother telephoned that evening.

'Darling, I have the most wonderful news. You'll be so thrilled—but I expect you've guessed already.'

'No, I haven't guessed anything.'

'Daddy and I are going to get married.'

'Married?'

'Isn't it wonderful? After all these years we've discovered that our love never really died. We were always meant to be together, and when that's true nothing can really keep you apart. Don't you agree?'

'I don't know,' Olivia whispered.

Luckily Melisande was too wrapped up in herself to hear this.

'We've both suffered so much, but it was all worth it to find each other again. The wedding is next Friday and I want you to be my bridesmaid.'

She should have been expecting this, but for some reason it came as a shock.

'Melly, I really don't think—'

'Oh, but, darling, it'll be so beautiful. Just think of it—true love rediscovered, and there, as my attendant, is the offspring of that love. Now, come along, don't be a miserable old grumpy. Of course you'll do it.'

'So I said yes,' Olivia told Norah next day. 'At least, she said yes, and I didn't have the energy to argue. Somehow I just can't take it seriously.'

'Oh, it's serious, all right,' Norah said caustically. 'You can't blame your mother. Time's getting on, and it was a very big win.'

'What was?'

'Your father had a win on the lottery some time back.'

'So that's where the cheque came from.'

'I'm glad he had the decency to give you some, even if it was just a way of shutting you up. He's rolling in it at the moment, which explains a lot about "love's young dream". Or, in their case, love's middle-aged dream.'

'Oh, heavens,' Olivia said, beginning to laugh.

She attended the elaborate wedding and endured the sight of her parents acting like skittering young lovers. At the reception almost everyone made speeches about the power of eternal love, and she wanted to cry out at the vulgar exhibition of something that to her was sacred. Afterwards Melisande embraced her dramatically.

'I'm so sorry you're here alone. Wasn't there some nice young man you could have brought? Well, better luck next time. We don't want you to be a miserable old maid, do we?'

'I suppose there are worse things than being alone,' Olivia observed mildly.

'Oh, no, my darling, I promise you there aren't.'

'I'm very happy for you, Mother.'

'You did promise not to call me that.'

Olivia's sense of humour came to her rescue.

'If I can't call my mother "Mother" on the day she marries my father, well, when can I?'

'Pardon?'

'Never mind. Goodbye, Mother. Have a happy marriage.'

Soon it would be the twenty-third of the month, the day on which Biyu had wanted her and Lang to marry. They had laughed at her determination, but now Olivia's heart ached to think of it.

'She's consoling herself with Wei's wedding,' Lang told her. 'He and Suyin were going to wait until autumn, but she ordered them to make it the twenty-third, so they did as they were told.'

Olivia dreaded the arrival of the day but it started with a pleasant surprise. Opening a parcel delivered by the postman, she discovered a butterfly brooch that exactly matched the one Lang had given her. On the card he'd written,

Do you need me to tell you that it's all still true? Call me as soon as this arrives, any time.

It was midnight in Beijing but he was there waiting for her.

'Thank heavens!' he said fervently. 'I've been praying I wouldn't miss your call.'

'You should be getting some rest,' she chided him fondly. 'You look tired.'

'I can't rest until I've talked to you. Tell me that you like it.'

'It was exactly what I needed.'

'Tell me that you still love me.'

'Yes, *sir*,' she said, giving him a mocking salute. 'I obey.'

'I'm sorry.' He grinned. 'I don't change, do I? Still giving orders.'

'Giving direct orders isn't really your way. You're better at pulling strings from behind. I guess you're just practising an autocratic manner for when you get the job. Has anything happened?'

'It'll be any day now. Darling, you still haven't told me that you love me.'

She was feeling lighthearted for the first time in weeks. 'Well,' she teased. 'Let me see…'

She was interrupted by the sound of his phone. He snatched it up, and immediately became angry.

'What, *now*? All right, I'm coming.' He turned back to the screen. 'That was the hospital. I have to go. We'll talk again tomorrow.'

'Lang, I—'

But he had gone.

She sat very still for a while, looking at the blank screen. Then she went to bed.

Next morning the doctor said to her, 'Norah can't be left on her own, but if you're going to live with her then I think we can send her home.'

'Yes, I'll always be there,' Olivia assured him quietly.

Norah was sent home that very afternoon. They hugged each other joyfully and settled down to chat, but almost at once Norah was too tired to continue. Olivia put her to bed and sat with her for a while, feeling the responsibility settle around her shoulders.

Lang came online early that night. One look at his beaming face told her everything.

'You got it!' she exclaimed.

'Yes, they confirmed it today. I now have a three-year contract at more money than I was earning before. I can afford a really nice home for you.'

Out of this only one thing stood out.

'You've already signed the contract?'

'I took the first chance before they changed

their mind. I only wish you could have been there with me to make everything perfect.'

So that was it. He'd committed himself finally and, by a cruel irony, he'd done it on the day Norah's return home had made her frailty even clearer than before. If anything more was needed to confirm that their feet were set on two different paths, this was it.

She smiled and congratulated him, told him of her happiness and then of her love. His look of joy was the same she'd seen before, as though nothing could ever change.

'I love you so much,' he told her. 'I can't wait for our life together to start.'

He parted with the words, 'Give Norah my love. Tell her to get well soon.'

'I will,' she promised.

To her relief, the connection broke. In another moment he would have seen that she was weeping, but he didn't see it, nor the way she reached out to touch the screen as though he were really there, then drew away quickly because he would never be there.

An hour later she looked in on Norah, who'd just awoken and was cheerful.

'Come and sit with me,' she said, patting the bed.

As Olivia sat down the light from the bedside lamp fell on the silver butterfly pinned to her shoulder.

'That's such a pretty brooch. I've noticed that you always wear it, so I guess it must be special.'

'Yes, it's very special,' Olivia said.

'Did *he* give it to you? Don't worry, I won't pry if it's a secret.'

'When have I ever kept secrets from you? Yes, Lang gave it to me at the airport when we said goodbye.'

She removed the butterfly and laid it in Norah's hand. The old woman drew it close and studied it intently.

'It's so beautiful,' she whispered. 'It must have a special meaning.'

'Butterflies are a symbol of eternal love, because of an old Chinese legend.'

She told the story of Liang Shanbo and Zhu Yingtai, how they had loved each other and been forced apart.

'When she stood before his tomb, it opened and enfolded her. A moment later two butterflies flew up and away into the sunset, together for ever.'

'Together for ever,' Norah whispered. 'Even death couldn't divide them. Oh, yes, that's how it is.'

'How have you endured all these years without him?' Olivia whispered.

'But, my dear, I haven't been without him. In my heart he has been with me always, waiting for me as Shanbo waited for Yingtai. When my time comes I shan't be afraid, because we will take wing together. You're very lucky to have Lang. He's a man of great understanding.'

'But what can come of it? How can I ever marry him? How could I have engaged myself to a man I'd known only a week or two? Of all the people to do such a daft thing, how could I?'

'But you mustn't give up hope. You've got your whole future ahead of you. I couldn't bear it if you sacrificed it for me. Please, my darling, don't spend your life in bitter regrets, as I have, always thinking how different it might have been if I'd only—' She broke off.

'But you couldn't have changed anything,' Olivia protested. 'He died in the army.'

'Yes, but…' Norah was silent a long time, but then she seemed to come to a resolution. 'I've told you so much about my love for Edward, but there's one thing I've never spoken of to you or anyone. Things were different fifty years ago. Couples were expected to wait for marriage before they made love.

'I loved Edward so much, and when he wanted us to make love I wanted it too, but I was afraid that he'd despise me afterwards. So we didn't. I was *sensible*. I could tell he was hurt, afraid I didn't love him enough. I told myself that I'd make it up to him when we were married.

'But in those days we still had National Service, and he had to finish his time before we could marry. He was sent abroad suddenly. It should just have been a short tour of duty but he was killed by a sniper, and the world ended for me. Night after night I wept, but it was too late. He'd died without really knowing how much I loved him. Oh, Edward, Edward, *forgive me*!'

Suddenly it might have happened yesterday, and she sobbed without restraint. Olivia gathered the old woman into her arms and her own tears fell. For years she'd thought she understood Norah's feelings, but now she realised she'd never guessed the yawning chasm of grief that had turned her life into a nightmare of emptiness.

When Norah's sobs had subsided Olivia controlled her own feelings and managed to say, 'But things are different these days. Lang and I have made love.'

'Then you know what you mean to each other, and you mustn't take any risks with that. Don't let me see you wishing every day that you could turn the clock back.'

'I've been thinking. I'm going back to China to clear out my apartment and talk to Mrs Wu. I'll see Lang again, talk to him. Maybe we can come to some arrangement with me dividing my time between China and here. If not, well…'

'Oh, no. You mustn't finish with him.'

'I'm not leaving you alone.'

'I'm not alone. There's the rest of the family.'

'Oh, yes, Mum and Dad prancing around like the world's their stage. The others who send you the occasional Christmas card. I have to be here at least some of the time. He'll understand.'

'Perhaps he'll return to England.'

'No.' Olivia set her jaw stubbornly. 'I'd never ask him. Besides, he's already signed a contract.'

She didn't mention the other reason; the story he'd told her about the woman he'd left rather than change course had carried a hidden warning.

'I fixate on something,' he'd said on another occasion, 'and I stick with it. It doesn't make me a nice person.'

She hadn't seen the warning then, but it was clear enough now.

She clung to the thought that they might still be together, that somehow life could be arranged so that she could divide her time between China and England. It was a wildly impractical idea, but it was all that stood between her and the abyss.

At night she slept with Ming Zhi in her arms, gripping her more tightly, more frantically every time, as though hoping to recover the caution and wisdom by which she'd always lived.

She'd prided herself on those qualities, but in the end they had failed to save her from falling in love so deeply that she belonged to him body and soul, for ever. She could almost have laughed at herself, but the laughter would be terrible and bitter.

She knew that Lang loved her. But he was the man he was, a man made of granite beneath a gentle surface.

His face came into her mind as she'd last seen it in real life, not merely on the screen: the sadness as they'd parted, the yearning look that had seemed to follow her. Then she thought of how he'd beamed when he'd told her he'd got the job. He would survive their parting—if there had to be a parting—because he had something else. And she would survive knowing that all was well with him.

That was as far as she dared to let herself think. But the temptation to see him once more, to lie in his arms one last time, was too great to be resisted. From it she would draw the strength to live a bleak life without him.

She hired an agency nurse, a pleasant young woman who got on well with Norah from the first moment. She moved into the apartment at once, leaving Olivia's mind at ease.

The only problem now was what to say to Lang when they next talked, but he solved that by texting her to say he would be at the hospital all night.

She texted back, informing him that she was coming to China.

That was how they communicated now.

CHAPTER TWELVE

THE taxi seemed to take for ever to get from Beijing Airport to the apartment, and Olivia had to pinch herself to stay awake. When at last she was in her room, she left a message on Norah's answer machine, saying that she'd arrived safely. Then she lay down, promising herself that it would be just for a moment, and awoke five hours later.

Soon she must text Lang. He would text back, telling her the first moment he could spare from his busy schedule. Somehow they would meet, she would put her plan to him and perhaps they would have a kind of disjointed future. Or perhaps not.

Exhausted from the flight, she could see only the dark side. He would refuse. He had another life now. He didn't need her.

One part of her—the common-sense part—reckoned it would have been wiser not to come here. They could have talked online and decided their future for good or ill.

But common sense—such a reliable ally in the past—failed her now. The yearning to be with him again was intolerable. To part without holding him just once more, without feeling his body against hers, inside hers, loving her as only he could love—this would have been more than she could bear.

She put her hands up over her face and a cry broke from her at the thought.

But she was a dragon lady, strong and resolute, one who faced whatever life threw at her no matter how painful. If love failed her she would have the memory of love to carry her through, and this one final night that she had promised herself.

There was a knock on the door. Throwing on a light robe, she hurried to it and called softly, 'Who's there?'

'It's me, Lang.'

She had the door open in a second. Then he was in the room, holding her fiercely, covering her face with passionate kisses, murmuring her name over and over.

'Olivia, Olivia, it's really you. Hold me—kiss me.'

'Yes, yes, I came because—'

'Hush,' he whispered. 'Don't let's talk, not yet.'

She couldn't reply. His mouth was over hers, silencing everything but sensation. He was right;

this wasn't the time for words. She wanted to belong to him again, and it was happening fast. He had the robe off in a moment, and then there was only the flimsy night dress, which suddenly wasn't there any more.

She tried to help him off with his clothes but there was no need. He was already moving faster than she could follow, and when he was naked she could understand why. His desire for her was straining his control. He almost tossed her onto the bed and fell on top of her, loving her with a fierce vigour that would have made her think he was a man staking his claim if she'd been capable of thought.

She'd forgotten how skilled he was with his mouth, his hands, his loins. But he reminded her again and again, demanding without mercy, but giving with no holding back.

Their final moment was explosive, leaving them both too drained to do anything but clasp each other and lie still. Lang's eyes were closed, and he might have fallen asleep. She tightened her arms about him in a passion of tenderness.

'I love you,' she whispered. 'You'll never know how much I love you because I don't think I can find the words. And perhaps you wouldn't believe me, because how can I explain it?'

'No need,' he murmured. 'Don't talk.'

He was right. No words now. She was back in her dream, where only he existed. Nothing else in the world. She slept.

She knew something had gone wrong when she awoke to find Lang sitting by the window. She'd dreamed of awakening in his arms, seeing his face looking down tenderly at hers. After their passionate love-making, he should have found it impossible to tear himself away.

But he sat there, seemingly oblivious to her, absorbed in a conversation on his mobile phone.

She lay back on the bed, stunned and disillusioned. It had never occurred to her that she was already on the fringe of his life.

At last he finished the call, turned and looked at her, smiling when he saw she was awake. He returned to the bed to take her eagerly into his arms.

'Thank you,' he said. 'Thank you for coming back to me. Let me look at you. I still can't believe you're actually here. Kiss me, kiss me.'

She did so, again and again.

He was the one to break the embrace, laughing and saying, 'If we don't stop now I'll have to make love to you again, and then I won't be able to give you my news.'

'What news?' she whispered.

'I'm coming back to live in England with you.'

'But—you can't. Your new job—'

'That was my boss at the hospital I was just talking to. I spoke to him yesterday, asking him to help me get out of the job. I knew it wouldn't be easy, so soon after signing a contract, but he said he'd do his best. It was between me and Guo Daiyu, and Guo might still be available.

'He just called me to say it's good news—Guo can start almost at once. I wanted to tell you last night but I didn't dare. There was still a chance that it wouldn't work out and I wanted to be sure first.

'In a couple of weeks I'll be free and we can leave together. We'll stay with Norah and look after her. And when—when she no longer needs us, we'll return to China.'

'But you'll lose the job when it means everything to you!' she cried.

'No, it is you that means everything to me. I'll do anything rather than risk losing you.'

'But you said—when you told me about Natalie—and how you couldn't put her first.'

'Of course I couldn't. Because she wasn't you. I parted from her because there was something I wanted more. But I can't part from you, because there is *nothing* I want more. Nor will there ever be. Do you remember I told you that first a man needs to understand himself? Through you I came to understand myself. I'd believed that no woman could ever mean so much that she could divert me from my path. But then I met you, and found that I was wrong. Only you mattered. We must get married at once. I won't take no for an answer.'

'Get married?' she whispered.

'I can't go on any longer without being married to you. If you don't become my wife, then my life will be empty and meaningless until its last moments. Don't you feel the same?'

'Oh, yes, *yes*! But you never said anything about coming to England before, and—'

'You never asked me,' he said, with a touch of reproach. 'But that's my fault. I talked so much about myself and what I wanted that I left you no space. The fact is that nothing matters to me except being with you. We'll come back one day, and there will be other jobs.'

'Not this one. You'll have to start again among strangers and lose what you've built up.'

He drew her close so that his lips hovered just over hers.

'Shut up!' he said, lowering his mouth.

It was a kiss full of tenderness, not passion. They had all they needed of passion, but for now it was a promise for the future that counted, and the peace that flooded them both.

There was a knock on the door. Lang released her and went to open it. Olivia heard murmuring for several minutes. When he returned, he was holding a paper.

'That was your landlord,' he said. 'I told him you were leaving this apartment today.' He showed her the paper.

'It's my final rent bill,' she said. 'Receipted.'

'I've just paid it. He wants you out fast, because he's got someone else ready to move in.'

'You've arranged all this?'

'Yes, so let's hurry up with your packing so that I can deliver you before I have to go to work.'

'And where exactly are you going to deliver me to?'

'To the family. You'll have my room until we're married in two weeks' time.'

'Now you're giving orders again. None of this new man stuff, respecting my right to make my own decisions?'

Gently he took hold of her shoulders. 'Olivia, darling, that's what I've been doing up until now, and look where it got us. No, this time I'm taking no risks. The family will keep their beady eyes on you and make sure you don't escape. Now, let's hurry so that I can deliver you into the hands of your gaolers and get to work.'

They found the family leaning out of the windows watching for his car, and by the time it drew up they were on the step, opening their arms to her, waving and cheering. Lang had to hurry away at once, pausing merely to tell them, 'Don't let her out of your sight, whatever you do.'

The women promptly formed a guard about Olivia, laughing to indicate that they were all sharing a joke. Yet it wasn't entirely a joke; Olivia knew. Lang had endured the loss of her once, but he couldn't endure it again, and now he was nervous when he was away from her.

'We have so much to do before the day,' Biyu said as they drank tea. 'We must talk about the big plans to be made.'

'Lang told me you'd already have everything planned down to the last detail,' Olivia told her.

'He's a cheeky devil,' Biyu said serenely. 'What does he know about anything important? Now, down to work. This is an album of pictures we took of Suyin's wedding. It was very traditional, very beautiful, and yours will be the same.'

'You think a traditional wedding would be right for me?' Olivia asked.

'Of course. What else?'

Leafing through the album, Olivia had to agree with her. Both bride and groom wore long satin robes of deep red, the symbol of joy. She was suddenly seized by the desire to see how handsome Lang would look in this wedding garb, which had an air of stately magnificence.

'Now, we have lots of shopping to do,' Biyu declared.

'You mean, you're actually going to let me out of the house?' Olivia joked. 'I thought you promised Lang that you wouldn't risk my running away.'

Biyu's eyes twinkled. 'Oh, but four of us will be with you at all times.'

'Why didn't I think of that?'

One of the little girls named Ting, who was about twelve years old, confided, 'If you escape we have to give Uncle Mitch his money back.'

'He's *paid* you to guard me?'

'Of course,' Ting declared. 'Twenty yuan a day. Each.'

'That's about two pounds. You're definitely being underpaid.'

'Also some sweet buns,' Ting admitted. 'If you escape we have to give them back—but we've eaten them, so please don't escape.'

Olivia doubled up with laughter. After her recent misery everything that was happening felt like a happy dream, one from which she prayed never to awaken.

In the end eight of them went out, since nobody was going to pass up a shopping expedition. There were gifts and favours to be bought for all the guests, most of whom would be family members making a special trip in from the country.

'Will there be many?' Olivia asked when they paused for tea.

'About a hundred,' Biyu said casually.

'There were only eighty for me,' Suyin said with a giggle. 'You're *much* more interesting, ever since the day he brought you home.'

'One thing I've always wanted to know,' Olivia said. 'When I was there with him that night, you were all so wonderful to me. I know you were being courteous to a guest—'

'But you sensed something more?' Biyu helped her out. 'It's true. Not every guest would have been shown the temple and told the things that you were. But we knew you were his future bride.'

'He *told* you that?'

'Not exactly. It was the way he spoke of you—with a note in his voice that had never been there before. He'd only known you a few days, but something was very different. He sounded a little shy, tentative—for the first time in his life, I'll swear. I don't think even he knew what he was giving away.

'We honoured you as his future wife so that you would know you were welcome in the family. These last few weeks, we've been holding our breath, hoping that things would come right.'

She became suddenly serious. 'You were able to walk away from him, but he wasn't able to walk away from you. That makes you the strong one.' She added quietly, 'Dragon Lady.'

'He told you about that?'

'Of course. If you only knew how proud of you he is! He is a strong man in every way but one— you are his weakness. Never forget that his need is greater than yours. It gives you power, but we all know you will never misuse that power, and we can give him into your hands with easy hearts and minds.'

'Thank you,' Olivia said softly, so deeply moved that she could hardly speak. 'I promise that I won't betray that trust.'

Biyu smiled. 'You didn't need to tell us that,' she said.

Arriving home, they plunged into a discussion of details. Biyu insisted that everything must be done properly.

'So we must first seek and obtain your parents' consent.'

'At my age'?' Olivia said, scandalised. 'Besides, they're on their honeymoon in the Bahamas. They won't be back for ages.'

'But there is your great-aunt Norah, whom Mitchell says is like a mother to you. He tells me that she likes him.'

'She certainly does.'

'Then she'll say yes when we talk tonight. You

must show me how to work this video link he talks about.'

Biyu was fascinated by the reality of it later. Norah was up and waiting, and she crowed with delight at the news. Olivia introduced her to the family members who were at home, and Biyu explained about the ceremony of consent that would take place that evening.

'Then I'll catch up on my sleep and be ready,' Norah said.

By eight o'clock that evening they were all gathered around the screen for her appearance. The first thing she did on seeing Lang was to raise her thumb triumphantly in the air. He responded with the same gesture, which made everyone else do the same.

Lang introduced Grandfather Tao, who greeted her solemnly, and embarked on a formal speech in which he praised the bride and groom—but especially the bride—finishing with, 'Do you give your consent to this marriage?'

Norah smiled and inclined her head, saying, 'I do give my consent, with all my heart. And I want to say how proud I am to be connected with such an honourable family.'

Everyone bowed to her. She was one of them now.

As Lang had said, Olivia was installed in his

room. He hadn't thought much further ahead than that, and it came as a shock to him when the young women of the house, determined to protect the bride's virtue, gathered outside her door, barring his entry.

'Very funny,' he said wryly to Olivia, who was doubled up with laughter.

'Well, we must do everything in the proper way,' she reminded him.

'And where am I supposed to sleep until the wedding? I have to move out of my own apartment in two days.'

'We can find you a couch somewhere in the north house,' Biyu promised him. 'It won't be for long. Now, you may kiss your bride a chaste goodnight and leave.'

Conscious of his family's eyes on him, he kissed her and departed hurriedly.

Had they been planning to remain in China, there would have been the ceremony of the bed, when a newly purchased matrimonial bed was installed. This had happened at the wedding of Wei and Suyin a few weeks earlier, and they were making their own bed available for the bridal couple on their wedding night.

The result was a modified version of the ceremony in which the bed was moved a few inches to symbolise installation, after which it was covered with various fruits, and the children of the family, symbols of fertility, scrambled to seize them.

These days Hai was in his element, conjuring fish from all directions, while Biyu took care of the rest of the banquet. Because the words for *eight* and *good luck* were similar it was customary to have eight dishes, not including dessert. Shark's fin soup, crab claws and as many fish as he could find formed the basis of the feast.

On the last night before the wedding Lang came to bid Olivia goodnight, and they strolled in the dark garden.

'When we next see each other it'll be at the wedding,' he said. 'No regrets?'

'Not if you have none.'

'None at all. Are you still worrying about the job?'

'How can I help it? You may have lost the chance of a lifetime.'

'There'll be other jobs,' Lang said.

'As good as the one you've given up?'

He frowned a little, troubled that she couldn't understand what was so simple to him.

'It doesn't matter,' he said. 'I made my choice, and it was the right one. While I have you, I have everything. Without you I have nothing. There was never really a choice at all.'

'That's what *he* said,' came a voice from the darkness.

They hadn't seen Biyu there. Now she came closer.

'He?' Olivia asked.

'Renshu,' Biyu replied. 'Those must have been his very words.'

'"While I have you, I have everything",' Lang repeated slowly. '"Without you, I have nothing". Yes, that's what he said to Jaio when he went to rescue her. And she understood that he meant every word and she could trust him never to have any regrets.'

He was looking at Olivia as he said this, a slight question in his eyes.

'Yes,' she said joyfully. 'She understood. It took her too long, but in the end she really understood.'

Biyu touched Lang's cheek.

'Congratulations,' she said. 'You are truly a son of Renshu.'

She drifted away into the darkness.

'That was it,' Olivia said. 'That's what you were waiting for, the moment of complete acceptance. It came in its own time.'

'As you said it would. You were right, as you are right about everything. I can safely put my fate in your hands, and tomorrow that is what I will do.'

He drew her close, not in a kiss but a hug. Their bodies pressed tightly together so that in the darkness they looked like one person. Looking back at them, Biyu smiled in satisfaction.

Because there were so many guests the wedding could not be held at home, and a hall had been booked two streets away.

Norah was with her as soon as she rose. Suyin made the connection and kept the camera on Olivia as they prepared her in her red-satin gown and dressed her hair in the style of a married woman, as she would soon become.

Norah watched it all in ecstasy. She had rested all day so that she would be fresh enough to stay up overnight, and now she and her nurse sat together, eyes fixed on the screen.

The groom, accompanied by the sound of drums and gongs, arrived in a sedan chair to collect his bride and take her to the place of the marriage. Olivia was pleased to see that he looked as splendidly handsome in traditional attire as she had known he would.

At this point there was a small delay. The groom requested that the bride appear but the bride's attendants, in accordance with tradition, refused to produce her until mollified by gifts. Since the attendants were the children of the house, there was a good deal of horse trading, led by Ting, and the price rose higher and higher.

'How are they doing?' Olivia asked Suyin from behind the window.

'Ting is driving a hard bargain,' Suyin chuckled. 'At this rate, you'll be lucky to be married today.'

At last Biyu intervened, declaring that enough was enough. The children seized their prizes and scampered away, squeaking with satisfaction.

Then it was time for the bride to get into her sedan chair for the journey to where the ceremony was to take place. All around her firecrackers exploded as she began her journey.

As they travelled she couldn't help thinking about Zhu Yingtai going to her wedding in a similar sedan, stopping it beside Liang Shanbo's grave and leaving it to join him for ever. It was in memory of this that Lang had given her the silver butterflies, and now she wore them both on her dress.

The wedding itself was simple. In the hall they approached the altar and spoke the words of homage to heaven and earth and the ancestors. There followed the declaration of homage to each other, expressed formally, but saying so much more than mere words could ever convey.

One of Lang's young cousins had undertaken to care for the laptop with the camera, and he did his duties so well that Norah saw everything close-up.

When the little ceremony was over the bride and groom bowed to each other. Now it was time for the feast. An elaborate paper dragon bounded into the room and performed a dance to loud applause. Then Suyin sang the song she had written in their honour:

'Now our family is happy
Because you are a part of us.
This you will always be,
Near or far.'

Hidden by the heavy red satin, Olivia reached out her hand for Lang's and felt him seize her in return. They both understood the message: near or far.

There was an extra touch that she hadn't expected but which filled her with happiness: Suyin went to stand before the camera and sang directly to Norah, repeating in English the words she had already sung, welcoming Norah as one of them.

Everyone saluted Norah, and she in turn raised a glass.

At last it was over. The crowds faded, the noise was silenced, darkness fell and they were finally alone.

'Are you happy?' Lang asked as they lay together.

'If this is the only happiness I ever know for the rest of my life,' she replied softly, 'it will be enough. I have everything.'

'And I shall give you everything in my power,' he vowed. 'All I ask is your love and your eternal presence.'

Her lips answered him silently, and after that nothing more was said.

They lingered two more days, paying visits of respect to those who had come in from distant places to be at their wedding. Then it was time to go. Everyone came to see them off at the airport.

Lang was very quiet, but sometimes his eyes rested on Olivia's shoulder where she had pinned the two butterflies, symbols of eternal love and fidelity. He was content.

At last the goodbyes were finished and they were on the aircraft, gliding down the runway, taking off.

Higher they climbed, and higher, with the ground falling away beneath them until they were in the clouds. Then the clouds too disappeared and they were up in the clear, brilliant air, still climbing. Olivia watched through the window, entranced by the beauty. But then…

She blinked and gave herself a little shake. She was dreaming; she must be. Because otherwise she could have sworn she saw two butterflies flying together.

That was impossible. No butterfly could climb

this high. When she looked back, the illusion would have disappeared.

But it persisted: two bright, darting creatures fluttering here and there, until at last they turned and winged their way towards the sun, blended with the air and vanished as if they had never been.

Full of wonder, she turned to Lang and found that he too was looking out of the window. Then he smiled at her and nodded.

Norah lived another eighteen months, finally dying peacefully with Olivia and Lang holding her hands.

She was cremated, and when they returned to China they took her ashes and laid them in the little temple with the ashes of Meihui.

Her photograph is there today, with one of Edward close by. They stand opposite the pictures of Meihui and John Mitchell.

Beside them are more pictures, of Lang, Olivia and their baby son.

Above them on the wall are written the words of the faith by which Jaio and Renshu lived two-thousand years ago, and which still survive in their descendants:

Love is the shield that protects us from harm.

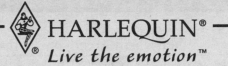

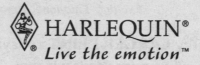

HARLEQUIN®
INTRIGUE®

BREATHTAKING ROMANTIC SUSPENSE

Shared dangers and passions lead to electrifying romance and heart-stopping suspense!

Every month, you'll meet six new heroes who are guaranteed to make your spine tingle and your pulse pound. With them you'll enter into the exciting world of Harlequin Intrigue— where your life is on the line and so is your heart!

THAT'S INTRIGUE—
ROMANTIC SUSPENSE
AT ITS BEST!

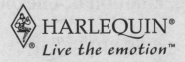

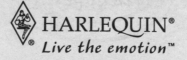

Harlequin® Historical
Historical Romantic Adventure!

*Imagine a time of chivalrous
knights and unconventional ladies,
roguish rakes and impetuous
heiresses, rugged cowboys
and spirited frontierswomen—
these rich and vivid tales will
capture your imagination!*

*Harlequin Historical . . .
they're too good to miss!*

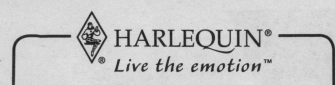